I0609754

KILLER MOVE

ERITIS BOOK II

T.E. STOUYER

Copyright © 2018 T.E. STOUYER

All rights reserved.

No part of this book may be reproduced, or stored in a
retrieval system, or transmitted in any form or by any means
(electronic, mechanical, photocopying, recording, or
otherwise) without prior written permission from the author,
except for the use of brief quotations in a book review.

This is a work of fiction. Names, characters, places,
organizations, businesses, events, and incidents either are the
products of the author's imagination or are used fictitiously.
Any resemblance to actual persons, living or dead, or actual
events is purely coincidental.

ISBN 978-1-9999649-6-2

"Whoever fights monsters should see to it that in the process they do not become a monster. And when you look long into an abyss, the abyss also looks into you."

FRIEDRICH NIETZSCHE, *Beyond Good and Evil*

ERITIS

PART TWO

Chapter 1 – Cryptic

"Aha! Found it!" said Arianne, in a louder voice than she had intended.

She carefully removed a small wooden box from the display cabinet and opened it.

A satisfied smile flashed across her lips. She was pleased to gaze upon her father's necklace once again.

"About time," Kincade whispered. "I was starting to think this would take all night."

"Well, excuse me, 'Mr. helpful'," she said, the tone of her voice also dropping to a whisper. "It's easy to criticize when you're just standing there, watching."

"Hey, you're the one who asked me not to touch anything," he retorted.

"That's because I was worried the cabinet doors might have been wired to set off an alarm. We had to be careful when opening them."

"So what? I can be careful."

"I know you're very good at what you do," Arianne said. "But … erm, how to put this … you don't strike me as the type of person who uses finesse to solve their problems."

Kincade frowned, looking offended. "What are you talking about? I'm all about finesse."

Arianne needed to bite her lower lip to stop herself from laughing. "Of course, sorry," she said.

"More seriously though, let's see that thing."

She took the necklace out of the box and held it up.

Kincade aimed his flashlight at the accessory and examined it.

The chain was made out of interlocked silver bits that converged on a pendant. The pendant itself was oval-shaped, with two distinct sides, and was affixed inside a thin metallic frame, running along its circumference. The stone was mainly emerald green, but blended with a nebulous multi-colored pattern that gave it an otherworldly appearance.

"Have a look at this," said Arianne.

She drew his attention to a small inscription on the pendant's metallic contour. It read, *'For Lucielle, to help her show the way'*.

"That's it?" Kincade said. "I thought this thing was supposed to help us find that memory card everyone's so interested in."

"It is," said Arianne.

"How does *this* help us accomplish *that*? Do you think the kid will be able to make sense of it?"

"No," Arianne replied without hesitation.

Kincade gave her a puzzled look. "No? Then why the hell did we go to the trouble of breaking into this place to get that necklace?"

"Shh, quiet," she whispered, worried that his voice had gotten a bit too loud. "The necklace is the key. My father told me so, himself. I just don't think we're meant to take the inscription literally."

"What do you mean?"

Arianne gave a coy smile. "Remember when we tried to contact Soran?"

"Sure. Why? Are you saying this is some kind of riddle?"

"Yes. It'd be typical of Adam to hide a clue in this manner. That way, even if someone saw it, they wouldn't think twice about it."

Kincade shrugged. "All right, I'll play along. Still, as far as clues go, this one's kinda vague."

"Adam's riddles are never what they appear to be at first glance. And the answers are usually so simple, they're very easy to miss."

"You mean he hides them in plain sight?"

"Exactly," she replied.

Kincade gave her a searching look. "You sound pretty sure of yourself."

"Don't forget," said Arianne. "My father asked me to hold on to this necklace until Lucielle became old enough to decide what to do with it. I had it for a long time before it was confiscated."

"OK, so what am I missing?"

"You'll see. Can I borrow your flashlight?" she asked.

"Sure," said Kincade.

Arianne returned the empty box to its place inside the cabinet, before she took the flashlight

Kincade handed to her. "Over there! Come with me," she said.

She led him to the back of the room and stopped between two large storage shelves, about five feet from the wall.

Once there, she raised the necklace to eye level and began to examine the stone. "I had an idea back when I was living at the Arc facility, but I never had a chance to test it. We were constantly being observed, so I couldn't risk it, on the off-chance I was right."

Kincade watched her attentively, trying to figure out what she was doing. "By the way," he said. "Are you aware that you keep changing the way you refer to Adam?"

Arianne turned and looked at him. "Do I? No, I hadn't noticed."

"Anyway, what are you doing?" he asked.

"Did you find anything strange about that sentence?" she asked as she resumed her curious task. "About the wording my ... Adam used?"

"How do you mean?"

"If this necklace is meant to help Lucielle find the memory card, wouldn't it make more sense for it to read: *'to help show her the way'*, instead of *'to help her show the way'*?"

Kincade thought about it. "Hmm … yeah, I guess."

"That's what made me think of something," Arianne said as she continued to scrutinize the jewel from different angles. "You've noticed that my siblings and I use a diminutive for Lucielle, right?"

"Of course. You call her 'Luce'."

"We picked it up from Adam. That's what he used to call her. Except in his case, even though it sounded like Luce, it was actually *Luz*." She said that last word with a Spanish accent.

Kincade had spent enough time in South America to acquire a working knowledge of Spanish. "He called her 'light'?"

"Yes. He used to say that she was the light of his life. Adam deeply cared for all his children, even Damien and Johann. But Lucielle was his favorite. I think part of the reason for it was that he had made her different from the rest of us, which makes her truly unique. It's also why we all feel so protective of her. That, and because she's much younger."

"All of you?" Kincade noted in an interrogative tone.

"Oh, yes," said Arianne. "The others would never hurt Lucielle. That night, Mitsuki was only trying to abduct her so that she wouldn't be able to help us."

"I see. But getting back to what you were doing …"

"Well, if you substitute Lucielle's name with the word 'light'… wait, I think I've got it."

Arianne pressed the flashlight against the pendant and then began moving the tip in tiny increments, thereby slightly changing the angle at which the beam traversed the emerald stone.

The stone refracted the beam passing through it and projected an intricate pattern of lights onto the wall and ceiling—it was almost like watching an indoor aurora borealis.

"It's the patterns inside," said Arianne.

"What about them?" Kincade asked as he marveled at the dazzling display.

"I don't think they're random."

"Not random? Then wha—" Kincade stopped short. To his utter amazement, he could see letters starting to form amidst the luminescent shapes. The words were still too blurry to make out, but those were definitely words. "Whoa!" he exclaimed.

After a little more tweaking by Arianne, distinct letters were shining brightly on the wall, and the pair found themselves staring at the verses of a poem.

From the top of a mighty tower,

A lone soldier gazes into the distance.

Meanwhile, the King in his castle chamber

Attends to matters of great importance.

Inside the chapel the candles burn

And the bishop ceremoniously sends a prayer.

All of them waiting for the Queen's return,

Along with the brave knights sent to protect her.

"Now *that* is cryptic!" a voice said as the bright ceiling lights flooded the room.

Arianne's body tensed up and a gasp escaped her. "Damien!"

Chapter 2 – Clash

The silver-haired man stood in the doorway with his finger still pressed against the light switch.

Kincade sized him up. *So, this is Damien,* he thought to himself.

"How did you know where to find us?" Arianne asked her brother.

"A little fox told me," he said. "Of course, I was already in London. I suspected the key was being kept in one of Leicester's offices. But I didn't know which one. And I had no idea what it looked like. I'm glad I made it in time to find you both still here."

"If you wanted to meet, you could've just called," Kincade joked. "And erm … a little fox told you? Don't you mean a little bird?"

"No," Damien bluntly replied.

"They have Nathalie Renard," Arianne explained—*Renard* is the French word for *Fox.* "What about Ashrem and the others?" she asked Damien.

"I imagine they're in all kinds of trouble by now," he replied.

"Don't worry," Kincade reassured her. "My team's gotten out of tough spots before. They'll be fine."

"Highly unlikely," Damien asserted. "None of you realize who Jenkins really is. If you did, you'd know there are plenty of reasons for you to be worried." He moved away from the door and casually began to inspect the various items inside the shelves with a vague interest. "I must have seen you with that necklace over a dozen times," he said to Arianne. "To think it contained a clue to the memory card's location. I wonder what Leicester would say if he knew he'd had it all along. I always assumed our father had left it to Lucielle for sentimental reasons. Something so important … he should have left it to me instead."

"That's just it, isn't it?" said Arianne. "He didn't."

Damien's eyebrows dipped into a severe frown. "Your point?"

Arianne stared him square in the eye. "You already know, but I'll say it anyway. Lucielle's the one Adam chose. He entrusted his legacy to her, not to you."

"She's just a child," Damien countered. "Some burdens are still too heavy for her to carry."

"For now, yes. But she will be ready, someday. Until that day comes, I'll look after her, and honor our father's last wish."

"And do you think our enemies will kindly sit around and wait during all that time? We need to act now."

"That's not your decision to make. Adam—"

"Adam isn't here anymore," Damien snapped. "As his true successor, the decision is now mine. This is your final warning, Arianne. Do not get in my way."

"Why does it always have to be like this with you?" Arianne bellowed. "Just once, I wish you'd try to be reasonable, Damien."

Kincade stared at the young woman. Her eyes were full of determination. But also sorrow, because she was so desperate to reach her brother.

But when Kincade turned his attention to the silver-haired man, he immediately knew Arianne's pleas would fall on deaf ears. He could sense a torrent of anger and hostility raging behind Damien's collected facade. Like violent waves crashing against the side of a cliff.

Arianne and her brother stood on separate shores, with a sea of diverging views and conflicting beliefs between them. At that moment, Kincade realized there would never be any possibility for the two siblings to find common ground.

Damien glared at Arianne, and said in a menacing tone of voice, "Hand it over."

She took a step forward and planted her feet squarely on the floor. "You know I can't do that."

"Perhaps you should both take it down a notch," Kincade suggested. "You guys haven't exactly been whispering up until now. At this rate, somebody's bound to hear us."

Arianne shook her head slightly. "He doesn't care."

Kincade raised an eyebrow at Damien. "You don't care?"

"You said it yourself, earlier," Arianne told Kincade. "The security measures here are minimal when Leicester's not around. There aren't that many guards patrolling the building. Certainly not enough to pose a threat to us."

"Then why did we try so hard to be discreet?" Kincade asked her, sounding perplexed.

Damien sneered. "The reason my sister didn't want to be discovered was not that she was afraid of being apprehended. She could have dealt with those guards all by herself. She was just trying to avoid unnecessary bloodshed." A barely perceptible smile appeared on Damien's face as he added, "I don't have that problem."

"In that case …" said Kincade.

The mercenary swiftly reached for his gun.

Now that it had become clear a confrontation was unavoidable, and considering the serious threat posed by this particular adversary, he had opted to make the first move. With the two siblings seemingly focused on each other, he figured it was his chance to catch the enemy off-guard.

But Damien had been expecting the attack. He pivoted his body by ninety degrees and drew his gun, all in the same motion, and at lightning-quick speed.

By the time Kincade leveled his firearm, he was already trailing by a tempo. And in a split-second, he realized his opponent would have the first shot.

Instinctively, he dived behind a cabinet as a bullet grazed his right flank.

Damn, he's fast, Kincade thought as he recovered into a crouching position.

Taking advantage of the opening created by her companion, Arianne sprang into action. Before Damien had time to turn his gun on her, she rushed him and kicked the weapon away.

The inevitable clash began.

It was the most astonishing hand-to-hand fight Kincade had ever witnessed. Both Damien and Arianne had obviously been trained in various combat techniques, but it was their speed and ferocity that kept him glued to his spot.

Despite everything he already knew about the genetically engineered siblings, Kincade couldn't help but be impressed and intimidated at the same time. It was like watching two wild animals trying to rip each other to shreds, but in a calculated manner.

Keeping his manly pride in check, the mercenary leader decided it was best to let Arianne handle the heavy lifting. Instead, he maintained a safe distance and raised his gun, waiting for his moment.

The two combatants bounced back and forth against the tall shelves, leaving flying shards of glass, cracked walls, and bent metal in their wake.

Arianne couldn't compete with her brother in raw power, she relied more on agility and technique, and tried to use her surroundings to her advantage. The problem was that Damien was almost as quick and agile as she was. As a result, the two of them kept disappearing and reappearing in the aisles, leaving Kincade without a clear target.

But despite not being able to keep a constant eye on her, Kincade could tell it was becoming increasingly difficult for Arianne to fend off her opponent's relentless assaults. She wouldn't last much longer on her own.

All of a sudden, a security guard showed up in the doorway, gun in hand. He spotted a man in a dark suit trading blows with a woman in a strange black outfit. He immediately aimed his weapon at them. "Hold it right there, you two!" he shouted.

The pair continued to fight. They disappeared inside a row of shelves, only to reappear a couple of seconds later.

"Freeze or I'll shoot," the guard shouted again.

They ignored him.

Having delivered his ultimatum, the security guard decided to make good on his threat. But just as he was about to fire, Kincade pounced from behind a cabinet and clocked him on the chin.

The guard was knocked out cold.

Kincade then cast a quick glance at the hallway door in the adjacent room.

No one else was there yet, but more security guards would surely be on their way. Maybe they could deal with the building's security personnel, but it was only a matter of time before outside reinforcements arrived.

He could no longer afford to wait.

The two siblings had once again vanished from his line of sight, but he could hear them fighting amongst the rows of tall furniture.

Considering the nature of the opponent, charging recklessly into the fray was probably not the wisest of ideas. Nevertheless, that's exactly what Kincade did.

But just as he started moving forward, Arianne was sent flying across the aisle.

Not wasting a second, the mercenary fired a couple of blind shots through a shelf, at the spot where he expected Damien would be.

But when he ran around the tall furniture and checked, no one was there.

"Behind you!" Arianne shouted as she lay on the floor several feet away.

Kincade promptly spun around.

He had no idea how, but Damien was now standing right in front of him. Reacting quickly, Kincade started to raise his gun. But his opponent gripped the muzzle before he could level it.

Assessing the situation in a heart-beat, the former soldier realized the worst course of action would be to engage in a struggle over the firearm. His opponent's unnatural strength would render any such attempt futile. Instead, he ejected the magazine and let go of the weapon.

Damien's face twitched in surprise.

This brief moment of hesitation created an opening for Kincade, who used it to land a strong left cross to his opponent's jaw.

Normally, this would have been a knock-out punch. But in this case, it was only enough to turn Damien's head and force him to take a step back.

What the hell was that? Kincade thought to himself, wondering whether he had just hit a person or a stone statue.

Since his punches were clearly not going to be effective, Kincade decided to try something else. He slithered behind his opponent, wrapped his left arm around Damien's neck, and interlocked his fingers to complete a choke hold.

That turned out to be a mistake.

This time, it was Kincade's face that twitched. He was shocked at how little resistance he could offer as Damien effortlessly broke free of the hold using plain brute strength.

The silver-haired man then flung his opponent upwards and slammed him against the ceiling.

The impact was so violent that the air was forced out of Kincade's lungs.

The mercenary dropped face down on the floor. But he didn't have time to catch his breath. He immediately gazed up and saw the sole of a shoe hovering above his head.

Damien intended to crush him as he would a bug.

Alert to the danger, Arianne charged at her brother, hoping to reach him in time to prevent the worst.

When he heard the rapid footsteps getting closer, Damien peered over his shoulder.

But Arianne had already closed the gap between them.

She jumped and bounced off the wall by pushing on it with her right leg. With one powerful thrust, she delivered a spinning kick to her brother's face, propelling him head first into a large shelf.

The heavy furniture tumbled over, dragging another two along with it, and leaving Damien buried under a sizable heap of paper, wood, and metal.

Kincade took a deep breath and then sprang to his feet. The gun's magazine still laid next to him.

But as he scanned the floor for his weapon, Arianne tugged him by the arm.

"Let's get out of here!" she said.

Kincade wasn't the type to run away from a fight. Not even from this one. Besides, he figured that, with Damien unarmed and momentarily out of play, if they could find either one of the two guns lying around somewhere, it would give them a decisive advantage.

But Arianne wasn't the least bit interested in debating the matter. She hauled her companion across the room so vigorously, he thought she would rip his arm clean off.

As they crossed the adjacent room and exited into the hallway, they heard a loud thump. No doubt the sound of an angered Damien overturning the shelves as he rose from under them.

Further down the hallway, echoes of loud voices and hurried footsteps were drawing closer by the second.

Arianne was right. It was time to go.

Chapter 3 – Bullies

The young boy stood in front of the blackboard holding a piece of chalk in his hand. He wore an unbuttoned shirt over a loose t-shirt, wrinkled pants, and muddied shoes. He looked indecisive as he stared with intense concentration at the numbers and symbols in front of him. His chin was slightly dropped and his eyebrows dipped into a serious frown.

He had been standing like this for almost ten seconds when a strident ring broke the silence.

"Phew." The boy let out a heavy sigh of relief. *Saved by the bell,* he said to himself.

"Very well, class, we'll finish the corrections tomorrow," said the teacher as her students started to bolt out the door. She took back the chalk from the boy standing at the blackboard and glowered at him. "As for you, young man, make sure you do your homework next time."

The boy said nothing. He calmly returned to his desk at the back of the classroom, collected his books, flung his backpack over his shoulder, and then left.

It was the afternoon recess, a time when swarms of children invaded the schoolyard.

Unlike some of the other kids who rushed down the stairs, skipping three or four steps with each stride, the boy slowly made his down to the ground floor. He didn't seem particularly excited to have some free time, and didn't appear too concerned by what was going on around him.

But as soon as he stepped onto the sand, a young girl came running towards him, waving her arms and shouting.

The girl had big blue eyes and brownish hair tied into two long pigtails hanging from either side of her small head. And her soft round cheeks were covered in freckles that ran across her tiny nose. She had on a yellow flowery dress that fell just below her knees and ended in white frills, and long white socks inside shiny black shoes.

"Richie! Richie!" the girl called out as she drew nearer.

"What is it, Laura?" the boy asked.

"It's David," she said.

"What did he do this time?"

"He took Stewie's new racing-car-thingy. I think those are a little silly but Stewie really likes them, and it's his new one."

"Where are they?"

The young girl turned around and pointed to one of the far-end corners of the schoolyard.

"All right, let's go," said the boy as he looked straight ahead.

He strode across the sand like a soldier marching to war, shoving aside all who happened to be in his path, and with his eyes fixed on a yet unseen enemy. Laura shuffled her little feet as she tried to keep up with him, despite making the occasional stop to apologize to those who had been bumped by her brutish companion.

When the two arrived at the far wall, they found an older boy and two of his acolytes taunting a smaller kid by dangling a toy car just outside of his reach.

"It's not funny, David. Give it back," the smaller boy cried.

"I warned you, Stewart. I told you to stop bringing those stupid toys to school, didn't I?"

"Alfred and Maggie wanted to see it. I was just showing it to them. Come on, give it back. My dad just bought it for me last week."

"Just tell him you lost it," said David. "And if you snitch on me, we'll beat you up every day after class until the summer holidays."

David Tucker was one of the oldest kids in the school—by virtue of having repeated a grade twice—and he was definitely the most hated. His favorite pastime consisted of harassing younger students, boys and girls alike. He particularly enjoyed playing humiliating pranks and confiscating toys, snacks, or anything else that might catch his eye. His reign of terror had been going on for over a year and a half now.

Recently, he had enlisted the help of other kids to carry out his reprehensible deeds. A couple of them were afflicted with a similar kind of mean stupidity as David, but the rest had joined him out of fear of reprisal. They figured that if they helped him torment other students, it would safeguard them from ending up on the receiving end of those mistreatments. It was a cowardly reasoning. But one that, thus far, had yielded the desired result.

With no one to challenge him over the months, and this being his final year before graduating to high-school, David Tucker had grown bolder and crueler.

At the beginning of the semester, a breeze of hope had passed through the school with the arrival of a new transfer student. He was considerably bigger than anyone else his age, and he always had a mean look on his face.

But not much was known about the newcomer. At first, a few boys had tried to strike up a conversation with him during PE, or in the canteen. But every one of them had been shut down in a radical manner. No one had dared to try after that.

The other students had hoped he might be the one to finally stand up to David and his gang, but their wish had never materialized. The new boy had made it abundantly clear he wanted nothing to do with anyone at the school. He almost always arrived late for class, invariably kept to himself during recess, and left as soon as the bell rang.

Only one other student had ever been seen talking to him. Laura Hall, a sixth-grader. Despite his intimidating size and scary expression, she seemed completely at ease with the new boy.

Eventually, the other kids noticed that on the few occasions the new transfer student made it to school on time, he always arrived together with Laura. And whenever it was time to go home, he always looked for her so that they would leave together.

It didn't take long for rumors to spread.

It was said that the boy was a child that Laura's father had had with another woman, and that since the woman had died, the boy had come to live with Laura and her family.

Coincidently, whoever had started that baseless rumor hadn't been too far off the mark. The boy had indeed moved into Laura's home. He was a foster child, placed with her family by social services after his previous foster parents had been arrested on drug charges.

For Laura's parents, the transition period had been fraught with difficulties. But for Laura, it had been a simple and smooth adjustment. Children sometimes have a way of breezing past such issues. She'd never had a brother before, and now she did. Besides, the boy was easy enough to get along with.

27

He mostly kept to himself, never touched her stuff, and the dog really liked him—a very significant marker for her. Both kids had accepted their new circumstances as if it were the most natural thing in the world.

"Hey, you! Give him back his stupid toy."

David Tucker froze. No student had ever dared to address him in such a dismissive tone before. He was so flabbergasted that it took him a moment to react and turn around. "Ah! You're that new guy. I've seen you around school. Since you're new, maybe you don't know how things work around here. I'm in charge. Nobody tells me what to do. Isn't that right, guys?"

The two behind him nodded and mumbled something in agreement.

The *new guy* approached them menacingly and said, "I won't ask again."

David recoiled. He wasn't used to being defied so openly. He sized up his challenger from top to bottom. The new kid must have had two or three inches on him. And he was much bulkier, but not from excess fat, his body simply appeared to have more volume.

David tried to stare down his challenger. But the boy wouldn't back down. He stared back at David with unflinching resolve.

During the course of his young life, the new kid had encountered his share of bullies. He knew they acted tough only when dealing with people far weaker than themselves, or when they enjoyed the advantage of vastly superior numbers. He believed them to be spineless creatures who always folded at the slightest sign of resistance. Especially, when dealing with an opposition on equal footing.

This bully was no exception. Despite the three-to-one advantage, David decided to avoid a direct confrontation. "There, you can have it back," he said as he pitched the toy at Stewart's feet. The miniature car hit the ground so hard that small fragments broke off.

"David Jeremiah Tucker, you can be such a jerk!" Laura shouted in anger. She went over to Stewart who had picked up his broken toy and helped him remove the dust from it. "Sorry about your car, Stewie," she said, trying to comfort her friend. "Come on, Richie, Let's g—"

When Laura turned around, she saw her foster-brother go after the three bullies as they walked away, looking pleased with themselves.

"Richie! Where are you going?" she called out.

The boy wasn't listening.

It had taken every iota of self-control he had to keep from bashing David's head the moment he had seen him. But that last spiteful act had pushed him over the edge. He grabbed the bully by the shoulder, turned him around, and gave him a long-overdue punch on the nose.

David fell on his backside and covered his face with his hands as he muttered some unintelligible threats.

He eventually looked around for his two acolytes, only to see their backs from a distance as they ran away.

Too cowardly to fight on his own, David tried to imitate his two light-footed companions. Unfortunately for him, the new boy wasn't the type to settle down easily once he got riled up. Despite Laura's pleas, he grabbed David by the back of his collar and belt, and tossed him into the sandbox a few feet away.

Chapter 4 – Rescue

As Rock flew parallel to the ground before crashing into a row of motorcycles parked on the curb, the long-forgotten memory from his middle-school days surged back to the surface.

As a child, Richard Reinhart had only gotten into very few fights. There had been no need. He had always been much bigger and much stronger than the other kids. He knew it, and so did they. So, no matter how strong the disagreements, or how high tensions mounted, it rarely escalated to the point of physical violence.

For a long time, he had believed that he had simply been growing up faster than the other kids but that they eventually would have caught up to him. But as the years went by, he had come to realize that it would not be the case. In fact, the opposite happened. The difference in size and strength between him and everybody else grew even further.

After he had joined the military, and later on, had teamed-up with Nate, Rock had often found himself engaged in hand-to-hand combat against several opponents at once. It had never been a problem for him. He was a force of nature.

But this time was different.

There was nothing natural about this particular foe.

As he lay on his back, Rock recalled the numerous times he had thrown someone against a wall, a table, or some other hard surface. This was the first time, as far back as he could remember, that he had been on the receiving end of such a rough treatment. His colossal size and considerable weight had always shielded him from this experience. *So, this is what it must have felt like?* he thought to himself. A faint smile escaped him as he hurried back to his feet. *I almost feel bad for all those poor bastards, now.*

He leapt away from the pile of two-wheelers, intending to rush back to Ashrem's aid, but a sharp pain to his right ribcage stopped him in his tracks.

"Ouch!" *I must have cracked a rib or two,* he thought. But he didn't have time to worry about such a *minor injury.*

A few feet away, in the middle of the road, the fight had taken a turn for the worse. Jenkins had his hands wrapped around Ashrem's throat.

The young man tried to break free, but his efforts were in vain. He sunk to his knees as his strength waned.

"Crap!" Rock exclaimed.

The murderous intent in Patrick Jenkins' eyes was unmistakable. He clearly meant to squeeze the life out of his opponent.

Rock dashed towards them, ignoring the pain shooting through his body with each step he took.

He tackled Jenkins like a defensive lineman charging a quarterback.

It was a strong impact. Strong enough to send Jenkins rolling back all the way to the curb.

Rock then knelt down to check on Ashrem.

The young man was unconscious, a few more seconds and he probably would have died.

Jenkins promptly got back to his feet and squared off against the giant. It wasn't every day he encountered someone capable of knocking him to the ground so easily, and this man had done it twice in the space of a few minutes. It was as though Jenkins was acknowledging Rock as a serious adversary. One that needed to be dealt with, the same as Ashrem.

Rock stood up and shot a quick glance at his companion. With Ashrem out of commission, making a run for it was not an option.

And just as the giant told himself their situation couldn't possibly be any worse, a black SUV turned the corner and screeched to a stop behind Jenkins.

Three masked men emerged from the vehicle, brandishing assault rifles.

They ran up to Jenkins and lined up next to him.

"What are your orders, sir?" one of them asked.

At that moment, Rock truly believed this was the end of the line. But when he took another look at Jenkins, he started to breathe easier.

The appearance of his men had prompted Jenkins to regain his composure. The rage that had been boiling inside of him a moment ago had vanished, or rather, had been contained once again.

"We're taking them with us," said Jenkins. "I have some questions for the big one. Get them into the vehicle."

The masked men were about to execute the order when, out of nowhere, Mitsuki showed up and shot one of them.

She had come from the direction of the hotel, just like the masked men. No doubt she had spotted Jenkins chasing after Rock and Ashrem, and had decided to follow him.

She fired at Jenkins next, but only managed to scrape him on the arm as he dived behind a light-colored sedan.

The remaining masked men immediately returned fire as they also headed for cover.

Mitsuki ducked behind the SUV and, holding a gun in each hand, continued to fire at Jenkins and his men, trying to keep them pinned down. "Get moving!" she shouted.

When Rock heard her child-like voice he wondered who she was talking to. It took him a second to realize she was actually talking to him. He had dithered at first because he had recognized her, and couldn't imagine she had come to rescue them. But that's exactly what she was doing.

In any case, this was his chance.

The giant flung Ashrem over his shoulder and darted into a side alley.

But instead of running away, he stopped and swiveled around to face the street. It wasn't that he particularly cared what happened to Mitsuki, or that he believed she had somehow become their ally. But the idea of abandoning someone who had just helped him out of a tight spot simply didn't sit well with him. He looked around, trying to come up with a way to help her in return.

There was a weapon lying in the middle of the road, next to the downed masked man. But it was too far. The other two would gun him down before he could get to it.

Jenkins spotted the giant standing in the shadows across the road, carrying Ashrem on his shoulder. He made a move towards them, but was immediately forced back by Mitsuki.

Meanwhile, the two masked men had begun maneuvering to flank the young woman's position.

"Why haven't you left yet?" Mitsuki shouted, in a poised but firm voice. "Get Ash out of here. Please."

It finally occurred to Rock that him lingering around only made the situation more difficult for her. "Dammit!" he cursed, his mind finally set on running away. But as he was about to leave, he met Jenkins' gaze.

For a brief moment, the two men silently stared at each other from across the road.

"Uh-oh," the giant said as he observed a change in Jenkins' expression.

Realizing he was about to lose his precious prisoners, Jenkins grew enraged. He placed his hands underneath the car that shielded him and flipped it on its side. Then, using only one hand, he pushed against the vehicle and spun it around by ninety degrees.

Rock gave a quizzical look. At this point, he was well past being surprised at Jenkins' inexplicable strength, but he didn't understand what the man hoped to accomplish. Granted, the car now covered half the width of the road, and provided greater protection from Mitsuki's frustrating blocking-fire, but it still wasn't enough to reach the other side. *Is he planning to make a run for it anyway?* Rock wondered.

Suddenly, the giant's eyes widened as he understood Jenkins' intention. He wasn't trying to cross the road. He wanted to retrieve the gun he had tossed away moments earlier. Jenkins couldn't get to his weapon before. But now, he could safely cross the nine or ten feet that separated him from it.

"Uh-oh," Rock said once again, but in a louder, more distressed tone of voice. He held on tightly to his load and took off.

The big mercenary was deceptively fast for a guy his size, due to the long strides he took with each step. By the time Jenkins recovered his gun and put the magazine back inside, Rock and Ashrem had vanished inside the dark alley.

Chapter 5 – Emergency

After rummaging through the upside-down van, Rock crawled back out of the vehicle, careful to avoid the shards of glass scattered around him. He emerged feet first from the passenger side—it was easier to get out from there since Jenkins had removed the door.

He had found his gun.

He quickly looked over it to make sure it wasn't jammed or hadn't otherwise been damaged during the crash.

Then, he got up and listened.

He could still hear an exchange of gunfire. *Good*, he thought. *That means she hasn't been captured or killed.*

Instead of running clear of Jenkins and his henchmen, the mercenary had circled around the block and returned to his crashed van. Now that he had gotten Ashrem away from the fighting, and recovered his handgun, he intended to go help Mitsuki.

But Rock could also hear the police sirens approaching from the hotel, in response to all the gunshots. It wouldn't be long before they arrived, making any rescue attempt on his part even more foolhardy.

"Argh, to hell with it!" the giant exclaimed. He glanced at Ashrem who was still unconscious—he had placed the young man on the curb with his back resting against a parking meter. "Hang in there, buddy, I'll be back in a sec."

But Rock had barely taken a few steps when he heard the horn of a vehicle.

He swiftly turned around, with his gun raised, and saw an ambulance drive up to him and stop in the middle of the road.

The ambulance's side door slid open and Doc Chen appeared. "Come on, Rock. Get in!"

"Doc! What are you …? Never mind that," said the giant. "We gotta go help the girl, she's—"

"What are you babbling on about?" Doc interrupted. "We came all the way back here to get you and Ashrem. Carson and his goons won't be far behind, and the police are converging on this area. We gotta go. Now!"

The giant hesitated for a second and said, "Argh, crap!" He tucked away his gun, ran to the curb to pick up Ashrem, and jumped into the back of the vehicle.

As soon as both men were inside, Doc slammed the door shut and the ambulance rocketed down the road.

"What happened to Da Costa?" Rock asked when he saw his comrade lying on his back with a bandage around his torso.

"We ran into a few problems at the hotel," said Doc. "He was shot during our escape."

"How bad is it?"

"It's bad," Doc replied in a grave voice.

"Your turn, big guy," said the driver. "What happened to Ash? Was it Darius?"

Rock turned his head and saw Soran shooting glances at him in the rear-view mirror.

"No, it was that rough-looking guy," said the giant. "The one who's supposed to track all of you down."

"Track us down? … you mean Jenkins?"

"Yeah, that's the one."

An expression of utter disbelief formed on Soran's face. "Jenkins did that? ... to Ashrem?" It sounded so unbelievable to the young man that he found it hard to even formulate the question.

"I know," said Rock. "I was just as shocked as you are. That Jenkins fellow is as tough as a tank. And he's got some major anger issues. I don't know what you guys did to him, but I don't think he likes you very much. He almost killed your brother for no good reason."

Soran turned silent. He kept his eyes fixed on the road as he tried to make sense of what he had just learned.

"You were saying something about a girl?" Doc asked.

Rock lowered his eyes. "Yeah, it's that little Asian chick. She's the reason I was able to get away. She asked me to get Ashrem outta there. I think she was still shooting it out with Jenkins and his men. That's why I wanted to go back for her."

Upon hearing this, Soran stomped on the brake so abruptly that his passengers at the back were sent tumbling towards the front of the vehicle.

Despite the heavy police presence, Doc's group had managed to leave the cordoned-off area and had made it into the general traffic. So when the ambulance suddenly stopped, the car behind it came to within inches of crashing into its rear bumper.

What followed was a loud chorus of car horns, until traffic eventually diverted around the halted vehicle. But this being Paris, the first few motorists didn't miss the opportunity to yell and curse at the irresponsible ambulance driver as they passed by.

A sentiment shared by someone inside the vehicle.

"What the hell, man?" Rock shouted at Soran.

"We have to go back," said the young man. "We can't leave Mitsuki there."

Doc had bumped his head against the back of the driver's seat, and was now right behind Soran. He turned around, half-stood up, and said, "Calm down."

"She'll get caught," said Soran. "Or worse."

"Please, calm down," Doc repeated. "Think about it for a second. The police were on their way. So was Carson and his men. And with Da Costa and Ashrem out of commission, it's just the three of us, now. If we rush in blindly, not only will we not save your sister, we'll end up getting captured as well."

Soran nodded towards Rock. "What about what he just said? What if Jenkins tries to kill her?"

"I don't think he will," Rock replied. "During our fight, it was like he lost control or something. But when his men arrived, he told them to take us prisoner. If he really wanted Ashrem dead, or me, they could have simply shot us on the spot."

Doc placed his hand on the young man's shoulder and said in a reassuring voice, "Leicester wants all of you back at that secret compound, right? And Jenkins takes his orders from Leicester. They won't hurt your sister. You'll have a chance to get her back."

Soran closed his eyes and took a deep breath. Then, he placed his hands on the wheel and got the ambulance moving again.

Doc gave the young man a tap on the shoulder, and then went to check on Da Costa.

After another quick examination, Doc looked up and said, "We need to get him to a hospital. Soon."

"A hospital?" Rock exclaimed. "For all we know, half the city could be looking for us. What if they arrest him?"

"We don't have a choice," said Doc. "The bullet's still inside. Someone needs to extract it and determine the extent of the internal damage."

"Can't you do it at the house?" Rock suggested. "I'm sure that old man will be able to help you."

"It's too far," said Doc. "He won't last that long."

"It's OK, guys," Da Costa said in a weak voice. "Just drop me off."

Rock frowned at his wounded comrade. "What do you mean *drop you off?*" He then turned to Doc. "We're not going to abandon him too, are we?"

"You said it yourself," Doc replied. "Half the city could be looking for us. What do you suggest we do? Hang around in the waiting room for hours, drinking coffee while we wait for him to get out of surgery?"

The giant pursed his lips and looked away. He knew his comrade was right.

"Do you know if there are any hospitals nearby?" Doc asked Soran.

"Yeah, there's one not far from here."

A short time later, the ambulance pulled into the parking lot of a hospital in Neuilly-sur-Seine—to the west of Paris—and stopped about fifty feet away from the emergency entrance.

Rock and Doc Chen alighted from the vehicle and carefully rolled Da Costa out on a gurney.

Soran got out as well, and went to help them.

"All right," said Doc as the gurney unfolded onto the concrete. "You guys wait here. I'll be back in a minute."

Rock nodded at his injured comrade and said, "Hang tight, man. We'll come back for you."

"I know," said Da Costa.

"Come on, we need to move," said Doc as he rolled the gurney towards the emergency entrance.

Rock followed the two men with his gaze as they went into the hospital. While Soran climbed into the back of the ambulance to check on Ashrem.

The on-guard receptionist looked up as the entrance doors slid open. When he saw a man in a black tuxedo pushing someone on a gurney, he jumped from his seat and ran around the counter to meet them.

"What happened?" the receptionist asked in French.

"Do you speak English?" Doc asked him.

"Yes."

"He was shot. He needs surgery."

At that moment, a female nurse walked into the reception area, holding two cups of coffee. At first, she paused in surprise when she found that her colleague was no longer at his post. Then, she jumped on the spot, nearly dropping her cups, when she saw him running towards her at full speed.

The receptionist rushed back to his counter and picked up a phone.

"What's going on?" the nurse asked, a little rattled.

"Someone was shot," the receptionist told her as he nodded towards the entrance.

She turned and saw the injured man and his companion.

Without saying another word, the nurse left her cups on the counter and ran back the way she had come.

Doc listened closely as the receptionist spoke into the phone with some urgency. Although his French wasn't good enough to exactly make out what the man was saying, Doc was still able to get the gist of it.

Just as the receptionist hung up the phone, the nurse returned, accompanied by two men in green scrubs.

"Did you talk to the doctor?" she asked.

"Yes," said the receptionist. "He'll meet you in the surgical unit."

Meanwhile, the men in scrubs had placed an oxygen mask over Da Costa's face and were setting up an IV for him.

"Don't worry," the nurse said to the man in the tuxedo. "We'll take good care of your friend."

Without waiting for a reply, she and her two colleagues in green scrubs rolled the patient away and disappeared into the hallway.

The receptionist approached Doc and said, "Can you tell me what happened?"

Doc explained that the injured man was a waiter at a hotel where he had attended an event. And that, as he was leaving, the waiter had run after him to return his wallet, which had fallen from his pocket. Next thing he knew, shots were fired and the waiter was hit. They were already near his car, so he had carried the waiter inside and had driven him to the hospital. When he had arrived, he had noticed an ambulance in the parking lot. He had taken a gurney from the vehicle and had used it to carry the waiter inside.

The hospital's staff had already been informed that there had been an incident at a prominent hotel in the district of *La Défense*—although they didn't know any of the details—so the receptionist accepted Doc's account of events without reservation.

Sensing the receptionist was satisfied with his explanation, Doc decided it was time to leave. His prolonged presence posed a risk to both him and Da Costa.

But as he started to walk away, the hospital employee motioned for him to wait. "If you don't mind, sir. I need you to fill out a form."

Doc feigned a twinge of annoyance as he pulled out his phone and checked the time. "I'm sorry," he said. "But I need to get going. I have a plane to catch."

"I understand, sir. But this will only take a minute. It's procedure."

The receptionist walked back to his counter and leaned over to grab the form. But as he picked up the sheet of paper stuck to the wooden clipboard, he heard the entrance doors slide open again.

He promptly turned around.

The man in the tuxedo was gone.

Chapter 6 – Hospital

Later that night, inside the same hospital, Doctor Philippe Laplace walked into the waiting area of his unit on the fifth floor. He was a plump man, in his mid-fifties, with short dark hair and a perfect tan, and he wore thin glasses.

When she saw him, Marie Heirtmeyer jumped out of her seat and rushed over to him.

"Doctor, I was told the surgery went well?" she asked in a pressing tone.

He smiled. "Yes, your friend will be fine. I just checked up on him. I'm sorry I didn't come to see you earlier, but I had another emergency."

Marie breathed a sigh of relief. "Oh, thank you, Doctor."

"You're welcome, Miss. He was very lucky. Five or six more centimeters to the right, and the blade would have punctured his heart."

"Can I see him?" she asked.

"Of course. As a matter of fact, he's been asking for you. Room 508. Turn left and follow the corridor all the way to the end. But please, keep it brief. He needs to rest."

She thanked the doctor once again and then headed down the hallway.

It was long past visiting hours, only a few night-shift employees—nurses and janitors—could be seen wandering around.

Marie arrived at a hallway junction.

There was a station tended by a man and a woman, who were chatting and giggling together. They barely glanced at the detective as she walked past them.

Marie proceeded straight down and arrived in front of room 508.

She paused for a long while before she finally knocked on the door.

"Come in," a weak voice answered.

Marie slowly opened the door and went inside.

The room was a little small, but not cramped, and had a large window covered by white blinders.

There were two single-beds, separated by an olive-green curtain, but only one of them was occupied. Next to each bed was a side drawer, a long-arm lamp, and a sliding tray table.

Hans was lying on the bed nearest to the entrance, tucked inside green and white sheets. There was a needle inserted into his right arm, attached to an IV bag filled with a transparent liquid.

"You should see the other guy," he joked.

"I'm so sorry, Hans," Marie said in a meek voice.

"Don't give me that, partner. You have nothing to be sorry for."

"How about almost getting you killed?"

"That wasn't your fault, Marie. Don't beat yourself up over it."

"We both know that's not true," she said.

"It's nobody's fault," Hans insisted. "No one could have anticipated that ... whatever that was. In all my years as a detective, I've never seen anything like it. Who were those guys? And how could they do ... what they did?"

Marie shook her head. "I don't know. I can't explain it, either."

They stared at each other in silence for a while.

Suddenly, Marie felt her purse vibrate. She took out her cell phone and checked the caller ID number.

"Let me guess," said Hans. "It's the pride of the Berlin Police Department."

Marie cracked a faint smile as she answered her phone. "What is it, Jordi?

…

You know I'm not here for sightseeing.

…

You were able to narrow down the location linked to the email? That's great!

…

Quimper? How do you spell that?

…

Don't worry, I'll find it. Thanks, Jordi. I really owe you one. What's that? Hans? He's erm …"

Marie considered telling Jordi that her partner had been stabbed, and that, having undergone surgery, he was now lying in a hospital bed.

But Hans pre-empted her before she committed the irreparable. "What's the matter?" he said, in as loud and steady a voice as he could manage. "Is Jordi starting to miss me already? Put him on speaker."

Hans had witnessed first-hand Jordi's flimsy poker face. It had taken a grand total of ninety seconds for him to get the IT technician to admit that Marie hadn't really gone on some random vacation.

He worried that if Jordi knew the kind of danger he and Marie had faced, the other detectives would see it on the technician's face. Which meant that everyone in the department would know about it by lunchtime the following day.

The two detectives would then be ordered back to Berlin without delay. And they would have to explain exactly how they were connected to a shooting that had taken place in the French capital. Not to mention they would also have to give a detailed account of the circumstances in which Hans had nearly lost his life.

Hans decided he wasn't ready to have this particular conversation with his chief. *People jumping across building rooftops … men flinging him up in the air as though he weighed no more than a grocery bag … knives flying around on their own …* absolutely not. At best, he'd be put on administrative leave long enough to have his head examined. At worst … well, no one in their right mind would think it's a good idea to let a person of questionable sanity roam the streets carrying a loaded gun.

Besides, Marie would be the one getting most of the blame. It was her idea to come to Paris, for what was essentially an unauthorized investigation. She had kept secret the fact that she knew the victim—Mr. Schmidt—personally, as well as other pieces of information relevant to the investigation into his murder. Not the least of which was an actual viable lead.

And her motive for all of this? Revenge, for the murder of her friend.

Never mind being dismissed from the police force, she stood a decent chance of ending up in jail.

Hans knew Marie's impulse to tell the truth was born out of concern for his well-being. She probably figured it would be safer for him to be taken back to

Berlin at the earliest possible time, regardless of the consequences for her. But he had no intention of letting his partner fall on her sword over a decision he himself had made. She had warned him that it was dangerous to stay. He had chosen to do so anyway.

He gazed up at her and shook his head.

She remained silent.

"Hey, I heard that," Jordi exclaimed over the speaker. "Tell that smart-ass I only asked because I wanted to make sure he didn't get lost on the way to France. I'm surprised he didn't end up in Belgium or Italy, instead."

"No, he's here," Marie replied in a tame voice.

"Good," said Jordi. "I feel better knowing someone else is there with you. Even if it's just Hans."

"Yeah," Marie said.

"All right, call me if you need anything else."

"I will. And Jordi … thanks again."

She hung up and stared absently at her phone.

Hans studied his partner for a moment. "I know what you're thinking, Marie. Normally, I wouldn't bother telling you not to go. But whatever's going on here is definitely not normal. It's far too dangerous."

She glanced at him but said nothing.

"Look," he continued. "I get that you and Schmidt were close. I get it, I really do. But I doubt he'd want you to risk your life on his account. Come to think of it, that's probably why he didn't tell you anything. He was trying to protect you."

"I know," she said, wearing a sad expression. "You don't understand, Hans. That night when I found him grieving the death of his friend. That night, I saw how scared he was. But I didn't do anything. I didn't tell anyone. In his own way, he tried to tell me that something bad was going to happen to him, but I didn't hear him. I didn't listen. And tonight … tonight, I came face-to-face with the man who killed him."

Hans placed his hand over his wound. "I know. I met him too."

"The killer … he said something … he said it was my fault. I need to know what he meant. I need to see this through."

"Even if it kills you?"

Marie didn't answer. She thought about her close call earlier that night. About the tip of the blade pressed against her chest. If it hadn't been for the killer's own associate, she would have most likely been killed.

"Don't worry, Hans," she said. "Now that I know what I'm up against, I'll be more careful. I promise."

The two exchanged a long look.

"Fine," Hans finally said. "Anyway, it's not like I could stop you in my current condition."

She gently touched him on the arm and smiled. "Thanks, Hans. I'll let you get some rest, now."

Marie started on her way out. But as she neared the door, she stopped and turned around.

"Don't worry about me," said Hans. "We used fake IDs, remember? No one here knows who I am. Besides, those guys could have finished me off if they wanted to. But they didn't. Clearly, they don't care what happens to me, one way or the other. You, on the other end …"

"I know … but they did let me go. Well, one of them did. It's OK, like I said, from now on, I'll be more careful."

Marie left Hans' room and went to the elevators opposite the nurses' station.

Doctor Laplace was waiting for her there.

"Ms. Vogel—that was the name she had given the hospital staff—could I have a quick word?" the doctor asked.

"Of course," she replied.

He steered her away from the nurses tending the station and said, "It's about your friend, Mr. Ritter."

"What about him?" she asked in a worried voice.

"I'm not sure how to put this," Doctor Laplace said, sounding uneasy. "Mr. Ritter told me that he was stabbed during a mugging. He said that a man tried to rob him, and that the stabbing was a result of the altercation that ensued when he tried to fight off the mugger."

"OK …"

"The problem I have is that the depth and the angle of the wound would seem to suggest that the

knife was thrown at Mr. Ritter from a distance.
Now, I can't be completely sure of course—"

"No, the knife wasn't thrown," she interrupted.

"Oh, you were there?"

"Yes, but I only saw it from afar. I was on my
way to meet him. It happened just as I was getting
out of my car."

"I see." The doctor gave her a long, searching
look, and then finally said, "In that case, have a good
night. If you want to come back tomorrow, visiting
hours are from 8 a.m."

"Actually, I don't know if I'll be back tomorrow.
There's an urgent matter I need to attend to." She
looked around briefly, and then headed over to the
nurses' station. She found a small piece of paper,
scribbled something on it, and then came back and
handed it to the doctor. "Here. It's my cell phone
number."

Doctor Laplace looked surprised. "We should
already have your number on file, Ms. Vogel. Didn't
someone ask you to fill out a form?"

"This is my personal number," she insisted.

The other phone number was a dummy she and Hans had set up just in case. It would invariably go to voicemail after a couple of rings. She wouldn't even know someone had called until she went online and checked her messages. It was the best way to make sure the number couldn't be used to track them.

The doctor took the piece of paper. "Very well, then."

"I would appreciate it if you kept this number to yourself," said Marie. "Please don't log it into the hospital records. It's my private line. I usually only give it to my close friends and relatives."

"Yes, of course," he said. "I understand. And here's my card, should you wish to get in touch with me."

"Thank you, Doctor," she said as she took the card and shook his hand.

Doctor Laplace watched her as she walked over to the elevator and entered the carriage. And he continued to stare absently at the elevator doors, even after she was gone. He had felt a strange vibe from her. She had tried her best to appear calm and collected, but he could tell something had shaken her profoundly. Of course, it was perfectly normal to feel anxious after such a dreadful ordeal. But his years of experience in dealing with victims of violent crimes told him there might be more to it.

He spaced out for a while longer, until one of the nurses called out to him.

"Doctor! ... Doctor!"

Chapter 7 – Children

"Doctor Whitmore!" a man in glasses shouted angrily as he barged into the lab. "I demand you put an end to this, immediately."

The lab was a vast and spacious room with light-blue walls and blue floor mats. The ceiling was made out of greyish sandstone tiles and was covered by an intricate pattern of plaster lights.

The room was divided into five stations thirty feet apart from one another. And each station was fitted with an electric medical bed surrounded by various high-tech equipment, including a computer panel with three overhead monitors and a PET scanner ring.

Three men in long white blouses were standing at the three stations farther away from the entrance—one at each station. And lying on the beds next to each of them was a child in a skin-tight black outfit.

The children were held down by straps wrapped around their wrists and ankles, and each one had over a dozen electrode-pads attached to their body.

They moaned in pain as the pads repeatedly discharged bursts of high-voltage electricity directly into their muscles.

Meanwhile, the men in white noted their observations and recorded various readings on their panels.

When the man in glasses burst into the lab, one of the men in white stepped away from his station and came to meet him. "Professor Fournier! What are you doing here? I thought that you and Professor Karpov were attending a conference in London this week."

Doctor Stanislas Whitmore was a short man with thinning grey hair. Though he was only in his mid-fifties, his gaunt face, emaciated body, and pale yellowish skin gave the impression that he was much older.

"I returned before the others because I didn't like the idea of leaving you here alone with no one to look over your shoulder," Fournier replied. "Now, perhaps you can answer your own question. What are you doing here? As one of the lead scientists on this project I demand an answer."

"Of course, Professor," said Whitmore. "We're merely testing their pain tolerance levels."

"And who gave you permission to even think about doing something like that?" Fournier shouted.

"My superiors in Washington sanctioned—"

"Your military puppeteers have no authority here," Fournier interrupted. "We have total autonomy regarding all testing procedures."

Whitmore clenched his teeth in frustration but tried to remain calm. "There's really no need for all of this unpleasantness," he said. "My experiments are just as valuable as the ones you and Professor Karpov—"

"You call this an experiment?" Fournier interrupted again, his face red with anger. "This … this perversion. Good heavens man, you're torturing children!"

"Children?" Whitmore said with a forced laugh. "They may look like children, but you and I both know they are not. They're freaks, monsters … aberrations that shouldn't even exist."

Fournier moved closer to Whitmore and looked him straight in the eye. "I see only one monster here."

"May I remind you, Professor, that since they've all failed to live up to their potential as reliable soldiers due to their … psychological deficiencies, we're now free to study their abnormal physical and physiological characteristics in more depth."

"Enough of this nonsense!" Fournier barked. "You, there," he called to one of Whitmore's assistants. "Shut off those cursed devices, immediately. I'm taking the children out of here."

The assistant turned to Whitmore, hesitant.

"Erm … perhaps a compromise then," Whitmore hissed. "You take the two boys and leave the girl here with me for another hour or two. She might not be as strong as the others but she seems to possess the highest pain threshold. It would be of—"

"Are you mad?" Fournier bellowed.

Suddenly, a loud scream resounded inside the lab, drawing everyone's attention.

It had come from the boy at the furthermost bed.

Fournier and Whitmore shot a questioning look at the assistant standing next to the child.

"I didn't do anything," the man in white promptly said.

The boy turned his head and glared at Whitmore. Then, he closed his fists and contracted every muscle in his body.

"Is he trying to …" the assistant started to formulate the question that had popped into everyone's mind.

They all knew what the child was trying to accomplish. But they also knew it was impossible, even for those children. They were certain of it. A certainty held together by the unbreakable restraints that tethered the boy to the metallic bed frame.

But when all four straps snapped at once as the boy curled up and brought his knees and forearms towards his chest, they all froze in stupefaction.

They had studied the children for over a decade, measuring their abilities and monitoring their progress in every way imaginable. Nothing in those studies suggested that this boy would be able to break free of those specially made harnesses. Not at his age. The scientists' brains needed time to integrate this new startling data. Like a computer needing to reboot after a major update.

The boy, on the other hand, wasted no time putting his freedom to use. He rolled on his shoulders, raised his legs over his head, and wrapped them around the neck of the man standing next to him.

"What are you—"

Before the assistant could finish his question, the boy crushed his skull against the bed frame.

The man died instantly.

At first, the scientists' curiosity had blinded them to the danger they now faced. But the sight of their dead colleague lying on the floor carried the threat to its rightful place: at the forefront of their immediate concerns.

The boy jumped off the bed and ran straight towards the man standing at the next station.

"Wait! Wait!" the man pleaded, raising both hands in front of him.

He would have had better luck talking down a charging bull.

The boy vaulted over the next bed and thrust his legs into the assistant's chest, knocking him hard against the panel.

Two down. One to go.

Whitmore had done the math as well. He dashed towards the exit in a frantic panic, yelling, "Guards! guards!"

The lab doors opened immediately, and six men in riot-control gears, complete with helmets, body pads, shields, batons, and tasers rushed into the room.

Whitmore was almost at the door. He slowed down and breathed in relief. Help had arrived, and the child was too far away to reach him in time.

But as he glanced over his shoulder, he saw an object spinning through the air and flying towards him at high speed.

The boy had ripped out a monitor from its supporting frame and had launched it at the doctor, turning the flat screen into a lethal Frisbee.

A stiff gasp escaped Whitmore just before impact.

Luckily for him, it wasn't a clean hit. The tall rack next to him had taken the brunt of the attack. But Whitmore was still hit with enough force to snap his head back and cause it bump violently against the wall.

He dropped to the floor, bloodied and unconscious.

The guards drew their tasers and took aim at the child, but Fournier quickly jumped in front of them.

"Hold it!" the professor shouted. He then turned to the boy and said, "Ashrem, Stop!"

But the boy was looking past him, and staring menacingly at the guards.

Fournier moved closer to the child, to the point where he masked the guards from his view. "Ashrem, please, calm down. It's over."

"I won't let him hurt my sister again," said Ashrem.

"I know, I know," said Fournier. He knelt down and put his hands on the boy's shoulders. "I won't let him hurt her either. I promise."

"What did we do wrong, Professor?" Ashrem asked. "Why are they doing this to us?" His anger had all but faded, giving way to a child's anguish and sorrow.

"You didn't do anything wrong, my boy. Not you, not your brothers, and not your sisters. None of you did anything wrong." Fournier wrapped his arms around the child and added with teary eyes, "I'm sorry, son. I'm so sorry for all of this."

Ashrem hugged the professor and began to weep as well.

The other two children had watched the whole incident in silence as they remained tied to their beds. The one at the nearest station lifted up his head. His blond locks fell to the sides, uncovering a strange grin.

"Eh-eh, nice. I didn't think you had it in you, Ash."

"That's enough, Johann!" Fournier chided.

Deep down, however, the professor felt the same way. Ashrem had always been a tame and gentle kid. Fournier had never once heard him so much as raise his voice in anger. Not even when Johann and Kadyna teased him relentlessly for being *too soft*. Though he did his best not to show it, the professor was genuinely astounded to find that the kindhearted Ashrem was capable of that level of brutality.

Fournier stood back up and ordered the guards to wait outside.

Their leader protested, citing protocol and regulations, as well as a basic concern for the professor's safety. But Fournier wouldn't hear of it. He ordered them out and told them to take Whitmore and his assistant—the one still alive—to the medical wing, and to remove the other assistant's body from the lab.

Once the guards had left, Fournier took Ashrem's hand as they went to free the other two children.

They unfastened Johann's restraints first since he was closest to them, and then moved on to the last station.

But as they neared the girl's bed, the professor stopped in his tracks.

Her large brown eyes were fixed on Ashrem. She had turned her head slightly and was staring unblinkingly at him.

Her face was devoid of all expressions. A porcelain doll.

At that moment, Jerome Fournier witnessed something he thought he would never see.

Mitsuki was crying.

Chapter 8 – Unexpected Visitor

A single tear ran down the young girl's cheek, sliding along her smooth skin until it reached the tip of her rounded chin. There, it hung for a brief moment, and then succumbed to the pull of gravity. And as it fell through the air on its fleeting journey, the tear formed into a perfectly-shaped sphere, before its short life ended in a splash against Ashrem's eyelid.

The young man woke up on a bed in Professor Fournier's home and saw Lucielle leaning over him with teary eyes.

"Ash! Ash! Are you awake?" the girl asked while shaking him with her tiny hands.

"Well, if he wasn't before, he certainly is now," said Soran who was standing next to her with his hands inside his jeans' pockets. "Don't worry, Luce. He'll be fine in a few days. You know how resilient we are."

As he passed through the upstairs lounge on his way to his room, Professor Fournier heard their voices. He stopped and knocked on their door.

Then, without waiting for an answer, he opened it and stepped inside.

"Ah! You're up, Ashrem. That's good," said the old man. "You look like you're doing much better."

"Yes, professor. I should recover soon," said Ashrem as he got out of bed.

But when the young man stood up and saw his reflection in the mirror, he froze and made a strange face. He was wearing silk purple pajamas covered in yellow pineapple motifs.

"I'm the one who chose it," said Lucielle. "I asked Soran to put it on you. It's nice, isn't it?"

Ashrem raised an eyebrow at his brother as if to say, *really?*

Soran grinned. "Hey, you look good, man."

"Erm … yes, it's really nice," said Ashrem. "Thank you, Luce."

"You're welcome," she replied, looking really pleased with herself.

"But I think I'd better get out of these, now that I'm up," Ashrem quickly added. He grabbed some clothes from the closet and went into the bathroom to change.

When Ashrem walked back out, he had slipped into a plain white t-shirt, khaki trousers, and a pair of grey sneakers.

"Are you sure you're OK," Lucielle asked, sounding concerned.

"I'm fine," he replied. "Like Soran said, we're resilient."

But despite Ashrem's claims to the contrary, the others could tell he still experienced some pain and discomfort from his injuries.

Even so, Professor Fournier smiled as he was really pleased to see the young man back on his feet. But then, all of a sudden, his smile froze awkwardly when he saw that the three siblings were intensely staring at him.

"What's wrong?" he asked them.

Soran took his hands out of his pockets and said in a grave tone, "There's something we need to ask you, Professor."

Fournier's smile had now completely vanished. It was never a good sign when Soran turned serious.

"It's about Jenkins," Soran continued.

"Hey, Pops! We need you downstairs," a voice shouted from the other side of the door, interrupting them.

Rock had rushed up the stairs and had called the professor from across the lounge.

Fournier promptly opened the door. "What's the matter?" he asked.

"Some chick's walking up to the house," said the mercenary.

"What? Who?" The old man asked, sounding surprised.

"What are you asking me for? It's your house," Rock threw back.

A troubled look appeared on Fournier's face. In all the time he had lived there, he had never once had a single unexpected visitor. And for good reason. He was in hiding. And considering everything that had happened recently, the timing of this first unannounced visit seemed a little too coincidental.

"All right, I'll go see who she is," he said. But as he left the room, he turned to the three siblings.

"You should all stay here. It's better if she doesn't see you." He then glanced at Rock and added, "That goes for you too, my oversized friend."

"I know, I know," the giant mumbled. "I'm too conspicuous. Doc said the same thing."

Fournier hurried down the stairs and found Doc and Sonar—Sean 'Sonar' Riley—waiting for him near the front door. "Shouldn't you two keep out of sight as well?" he asked them.

"I don't know," Sonar replied. "She's been checking out the house from a distance for the past five minutes, at least. I'm sure she knows you're not alone."

"I'll stay with the professor," said Doc. "Sonar, you keep an eye out, in case she brought someone else with her."

"Roger that," said the redhead. He left the two men at the entrance and disappeared in the hallway as he headed to the back.

"Five minutes, huh? That's odd," said Fournier as he peeked through the small window by the door.

"Recognize her?" Doc asked.

The old man took another look at the tall blond woman in the grey pantsuit who was cautiously walking towards the house. "No, I've never seen her before in my life."

The woman finally arrived at the porch and rang the bell.

Fournier waited a moment and then opened the door. "Yes?"

She paused and studied him with a strange expression, as if she was trying to recognize him. "Professor Jerome Fournier?" she asked.

The professor felt a chill run down his spine. She knew his real name, not the alias he had been using for the past few years. He had left the name Jerome Fournier behind when he had fled from the Arc facility and had never used it since. *How could she know it?*

The old man tried to keep a straight face and said, "Sorry, you've got the wrong address. There's no one here by that name."

"Please, I need to speak with you," she insisted.

"I told you, you've got the wrong place. Goodbye, Miss," he said, before shutting the door in her face.

"I was a friend of Professor Aleksandr Karpov," she shouted from the other side.

After a brief period of silence, the door opened again.

"Who are you?" Fournier asked.

"My name is Marie Heirtmeyer. I'm only asking for a few minutes of your time. Please."

Fournier hesitated a moment, and then stepped aside and nodded for her to come in.

Marie proceeded with caution—the events of the previous night had made her unusually wary. She halted as soon as she saw Doc standing in the hallway.

Fournier simply introduced him as a friend, without giving his name, and then led them into the living room.

Marie waited for the two men to take their seats before taking hers. She chose the one nearest to the door, opposite Doc, with the professor to her left, and with a clear view of the hallway to her right.

"Well, Miss, what can I do for you?" Fournier asked.

Marie shot a quick glance at Doc and seemed to hesitate.

"It's all right," said Fournier. "You can speak freely. You said your name was Marie …"

"Heirtmeyer, yes."

"And how is it you've come to know my name?"

"I'm a detective in the Criminal Investigation Division in Berlin."

"Berlin?" Fournier echoed.

"Yes. I met Professor Karpov during one of my investigations. He actually solved that case for me." An affectionate smile flickered across her face. "Anyway, long story short, we became friends. Close friends. We spent a lot of time together, and I cared for him very much."

Fournier raised his chin and examined her from behind his glasses. "That still doesn't explain how you know my name. Or Alek's, for that matter. I'm quite certain he would never have revealed it to anyone."

"Oh, he didn't," said Marie. "At least not intentionally." She took out two photographs from her purse and handed one to the old man.

It was the picture Marie had seen on the night she had learned of Aleksandr Karpov's true identity. A picture of three men standing together, smiling.

"You look about fifteen to twenty years younger in that photograph," Marie said. "But it's definitely you, with Professor Karpov, and that French diplomat who died in a car accident. Except, the professor told me his friend's death was no accident. He was convinced someone was behind the whole thing, and that the same people would come for him too." Marie lowered her eyes. "I believed him, of course, but I didn't take the threat seriously enough. And now he's gone."

Deep furrows formed on Fournier's brow as he paused to think.

Up until then, Doc had listened in silence as he observed the young woman. His instincts told him she was being truthful, but experience had taught him that one could never be too careful. "Why should we believe any of this?" He asked her. "For all we know, Karpov never gave you this photograph. You said you're a detective? You could have just found it inside his apartment."

"I did find it," she said. "The professor would never have let me take it. He was far too paranoid."

She handed the second photograph to Fournier. It was the one taken in a park by an old Japanese couple. It showed Marie and Professor Karpov holding each other by the arm. They were both smiling. And it wasn't the kind of fake smile people make when they know their picture is about to be taken. Those were genuine, carefree smiles.

Fournier's throat tightened with emotion when he gazed at the picture. He didn't think neither he nor his friend would ever again be capable of displaying such a smile.

Just like Aleksandr Karpov, Jerome Fournier too had been forced to live the life of a recluse. He had kept a low profile, never allowing himself to form any kind of significant attachment to anyone. It was a life of loneliness, spent trapped in the mistakes of the past, and haunted by its many regrets. And yet, somehow, his friend had apparently managed to find moments of joy from within the confines of this isolation. It warmed Fournier's heart to see it.

He stared at the photograph for a long while, and then finally looked up at the young woman and asked, "How did you find me?"

"The email address," she replied. "The one set up for you and Professor Karpov. It led me to this area. And since I knew what you look like from the picture, well … I am a detective after all."

"I see," Fournier simply said.

"This is not good," Doc remarked. "If she could find you, then it's only a matter of time before someone else does too."

"I kept the email secret," said Marie. "Only two of my colleagues know about it, and they can be trusted not to say anything."

"Why did you come here?" Fournier asked.

She locked eyes with him. "I want to find the people responsible for the professor's murder."

Fournier jumped in his seat. "What? No, no, no, no, that's a bad idea."

"A *very* bad idea," Doc emphasized. "You don't want to get mixed up in this, trust me. You should go back to Berlin while you still can."

"Yes, yes!" Fournier vibrantly approved. "You should go back. Today. Right now. I assure you, it's for the best."

"I'm not going to do that," Marie told them in a firm voice.

"Young woman, you have no idea what you'd be getting yourself into," Fournier warned.

"You're right, I didn't," she said. "But I think I'm starting to, now."

"What does that mean?" Doc asked.

"Last night, I had an encounter with the man who murdered Professor Karpov. He nearly killed my partner. And he tried to kill me too."

Both men froze and gave her an incredulous look.

Seeing that they didn't believe her, she described the man to them. "A little over 6 feet tall, thin but athletic build, blond hair, blue eyes, pale skin, and a really creepy smile."

"It can't be …" The old man muttered.

"Actually," Marie continued. "I was hoping you'd be able to help me make sense of a few things. I get to see plenty of weird stuff in my line of work, but what happened last night … was impossible."

All of sudden, a redheaded man carrying a semi-automatic rifle came rushing in from the dining room.

Marie sprang from her seat, drew a gun from her hip holster, and pointed it at him.

Doc and Fournier also rose to their feet when they saw him.

The redhead put his hands up in a non-threatening gesture, letting his rifle hang by a strap over his shoulder. "Relax, lady," he said. "Believe me, it's not me you need to worry about, right now."

"What's up, Sonar?" Doc asked.

"We've got company."

Doc immediately ran to the window by the door. "How many?"

"Not sure," said Sonar. "Maybe a dozen. There are more of them approaching from the back."

Marie watched uncomprehendingly, her weapon still trained on the redhead.

"Friends of yours?" Doc asked her.

She hesitated briefly before joining him at the window.

Keeping her gun in her hand, ready to fire at Doc or Sonar at the first sign of trouble, she pushed the curtain aside just enough to see what was going on outside.

She didn't see anyone.

"Not there," said Doc. "Look farther."

Marie redirected her gaze. Before long, she was able to make out a number of dark figures shuffling inside the bushes.

"Who are they?" she asked.

"That's what *we*'d like to know," said Sonar.

"They're trouble," Doc said as he moved away from the window. "I'm pretty sure I just spotted Carson."

"Who's Carson?" the detective asked.

"He's bad news," Doc replied. "We have to warn the others."

Chapter 9 – Surrounded

A few minutes earlier, upstairs in Ashrem's room …

"It's no use," said Soran, his forehead pressed against the glass as he gazed outside. "I can't see her anymore."

"I told you," said Lucielle. "There's no way to get a clear view of the porch from this angle. Anyway, she's probably inside the house by now."

"I don't get why we all have to stay up here," the young man complained as he moved away from the window. "It's not like she knows who we are."

"We don't know who she is, either," said Lucielle. "Besides, the three of us should avoid being seen as much as possible." She then turned to Rock. "And you obviously stand out too much. You're too easy to remember."

"Huh! Look who's talking," the giant scoffed.

"Humph!" The young girl crossed her arms and pouted.

"What?" Rock exclaimed all of a sudden. It was the third time in the past minute alone that he had caught Ashrem casting a furtive glance at him.

The young man looked embarrassed. "Erm … I just wanted to say …"

"Come on, spit it out already," said the giant. "What do you want?"

"I didn't get a chance to thank you for what you did," said Ashrem. "You risked your life to save me."

"What do you mean, Ash?" Soran asked, looking intrigued.

"Last night, he had plenty of opportunities to make a run for it. It was me Jenkins wanted. But even after I told him to leave, Rock chose to stay and fight rather than save himself." Ashrem turned to the giant, "I'm ashamed to admit it, but I didn't expect that from you. You have my gratitude."

Soran laughed and gave the mercenary a vigorous tap on the chest with the back of his hand. "Look at you! After all that stuff you said about handing us over to Leicester. I gotta say I'm surprised. I guess I had you pegged wrong, big guy."

"Shut up!" Rock said as he shoved Soran back to the window.

"Well, I'm not surprised." Lucielle got up from her chair and walked over to the giant. "Thank you for helping my brother," she said in a serious tone. "I knew that really … really deep down, you were a nice guy."

"Did you have to say 'really' twice?" Rock complained.

"Uh-oh!" Soran suddenly exclaimed.

They all turned to the young man and saw him staring intently out the window.

"What did you make that noise for?" Rock asked.

"Everyone, get down!" Soran shouted as he dived to protect Lucielle.

Rock and Ashrem heeded the warning and quickly hit the deck just before a bullet smashed the window and shattered the light bulb on the ceiling.

The mercenary promptly drew his firearm. "Who's shooting at us?" he asked.

"I think they're Jenkins' men," Soran replied.

"How the hell did they find this place?"

A barrage of bullets tore through the living room for almost five seconds, and then stopped as abruptly as it had started.

"What's going on?" Marie shouted as she lay flat on the floor—along with the three men.

"No time to explain," said Doc. He gave a sweeping look around, pausing for a moment as he stared at the big hole left by the shattered glass bay doors. "We need to get upstairs."

"I agree," said Sonar. "There's no way we can hold this position. They'll overrun us in seconds."

"And how do you both suggest we get up there?" Fournier asked. "Won't they start shooting again if they see us move?"

Doc Chen raised an eyebrow at the professor. "You seem pretty calm considering the circumstances."

The old man chuckled. "I haven't had any real excitement in years. I actually find this quite exhilarating."

Sonar smiled. "Whatever, Pops. Just try not to get killed, OK."

Marie stared, wide-eyed, at the trio. "How can all of you joke at a time like this?" she said. "There are people out there trying to kill us."

"Yeah, we get that a lot," said Sonar.

"Yo! Is everybody alive down there?" A voice shouted from the top of the staircase.

Doc crawled to the hallway door and shouted back, "We're fine, Rock. And you guys?"

"Still in one piece."

"Good. We need you to lay down some cover fire so we can get up there."

"You wanna come up?" said the giant, sounding surprised. "Shouldn't we be looking for a way out, instead?"

"We're surrounded," Doc bellowed. "Just do it."

"All right, all right."

Rock hurried to his room to grab a black sports bag, and then returned to Ashrem's room and dropped it on the floor.

"What's in the bag?" Soran asked.

"I'm glad you asked," said the mercenary. He unzipped the bag and pulled out an assault rifle.

Soran took a look inside and whistled. "You've got a small arsenal in there," he said.

"Just grab something," Rock told him. "Hurry up."

The young man took out a pair of handguns and some extra clips.

Both men then took position by the window and observed the assailants as they methodically moved in on the house.

"We're not dealing with amateurs," said Rock. "They're taking their time, and keeping their exposure to a minimum, because they know we're not going anywhere."

"If all of them make it inside, we're in serious trouble," said Soran.

"I'll help too," said Ashrem. He bent down and reached inside the bag. But when he tried to straighten up, he grimaced in pain and dropped the weapon he had picked up.

"No offense, buddy," said Rock. "But you don't look like you're in any shape to help anyone, right now."

"Don't worry, Ash," said Soran. "We'll handle it." He then turned to Lucielle. "And you, stay close to him, understood?"

The young girl took Ashrem's hand and nodded.

Soran looked at Rock and asked, "Shouldn't one of us cover the back of the house?"

"No," the mercenary replied. "Our goal is to help the others make it up here safely. The staircase is on this side. We'll be more effective if we stick together."

Meanwhile in the living room, the small group had clustered at the hallway entrance, making sure to keep their heads down. They were preparing to make a run for the staircase, which was less than fifteen feet away from them.

Doc turned to Marie and the professor. "Once the shooting starts, run. Don't stop, and don't look back."

"What about you?" Marie asked.

"We'll be right behind you," he said. "All right, everyone ready?"

Three heads nodded.

"OK, Now!" Doc shouted.

"That's our cue," said Rock.

He and Soran immediately engaged the assailants from their high vantage point.

At the same time, Professor Fournier began to run as quickly as he could, closely followed by the detective. The pair rushed up the steps and ducked into a corner as soon as they made it to the second-floor lounge.

Doc and Sonar had been covering the other end of the hallway, in case the enemy entered the house from the back. But once Marie and the professor reached the second floor, they decided it was time for them to move.

Sonar was the first to arrive at the staircase, but as he circled the post and started up the steps, he saw four men charge around the hallway corner. "Behind you, Doc!" he shouted.

Reacting quickly, Doc knelt down, half-turned. He placed one hand on the ground to balance himself. And with the other, he leveled his gun behind him and took down the first assailant.

Sonar wasted no time backing up his comrade. He leaned over the railings and opened fire on the three remaining men with his semi-automatic rifle.

The assailants retreated behind the corner and returned fire.

While still shooting, Doc and Sonar hustled up the stairs.

When the two mercenaries made it to the second-floor, Marie and the professor came to meet them.

"Are you both OK?" Doc asked.

"Yes, I'm quite all right, thank you," Fournier replied, in a disturbingly cheerful tone.

Marie nodded.

The detective was still trying to figure out what was going on. Ever since the previous night, nothing seemed to make sense anymore. She had come to this house in search of answers, but instead, each moment she spent there pulled her deeper into a labyrinth of confusion. A confusion which grew even further when she saw a child with silver-gray hair and a huge man come out from one of the rooms, accompanied by two other men.

"So, who's the babe?" Soran asked as he ogled the detective.

Marie raised her eyebrows at him, surprised by his carefree attitude given their predicament. *Did I come to a madhouse?* She wondered. And come to think of it, now that she saw him up close, she thought this one too had an unusual appearance, with his different-colored eyes and short salt-and-pepper hair.

"Not now, Soran," said Doc. He then turned to Rock. "Good job laying down that cover fire."

"Thanks," said the giant. "But it was odd. They didn't shoot back at us, for some reason."

Doc Chen and Sonar exchanged a surprised look.

"Really?" said the redhead. "Well, lucky you. They didn't seem to mind taking shots at me and Doc."

But there was no time to ponder the giant's intriguing observation. The group could now hear the sounds of multiple footsteps scrambling around the ground floor. The assailants were inside the house.

The three mercenaries took position near the top of the stairs and prepared for the enemy's impending charge. Soran and Marie stood right behind them, ready to provide support, while the others remained huddled near the center of the room.

Chapter 10 – Ultimatum

"Jonathan Kincade!" a voice shouted from below.

There was a moment of silence as all members of the party upstairs exchanged startled looks.

"Jonathan Kincade!" the voice shouted again.

"He's not here right now," Rock shouted back. "Would you like to leave a message?"

"This is no time for your usual nonsense," his redheaded comrade told him.

"How about Hulin Chen?" the voice asked.

Doc cautiously leaned over the banister. "What can I do for you?"

A man appeared at the base of the stairs. "We meet again, Mr. Chen," he said. "I didn't get a chance to properly introduce myself the first time. My name's Randall Carson. I work for Mr. Leicester."

"I know who you are."

"Good, it'll make things simpler. Listen, you're outnumbered and outgunned, and there's nowhere for you to go."

"Even if that were true," said Doc. "After all those gunshots, I'd say there's a good chance the police are on their way here, by now. We could just hold out until they arrive. At which point, each of us will get to tell their story. I don't mind either way. But I'm guessing that's something your employer would very much like to avoid."

"Nice try," said Carson. "But I don't think you're eager to end up in police custody. Not that it matters. You and I both know there's no one around for miles. The police aren't coming. But more of my men are."

Rock turned to the professor and whispered, "Did you have to live in the middle of nowhere?"

"That was the whole point," said Fournier. "I was in hiding."

"Like I said," Carson continued. "You don't have any outs. We could set the house on fire and shoot down anyone who tries to leave, or we could just sit back and wait for the rest of my men to arrive."

"And yet," said Doc, "here we are, talking. Why is that?"

"Either one of those options would result in casualties on both sides, especially on yours. In fact, it's doubtful any of you would make it out alive. I don't want that, and neither do you."

"What do you propose?" Doc asked.

"My employer gave me strict instructions to avoid bloodshed whenever possible. If you hand over the analyst and the fugitives, we'll let your team go free. You have my word."

"The professor comes with us too!" another voice shouted from below.

"Ah, I see you've found our guest," said Doc.

Carson's men had freed the prisoner held in the basement. Mark Stanwell—Leicester's assistant— was fuming about the treatment he had received. There was a lot he wanted to get off his chest. He was about to voice his outrage at his former captors, but Carson silenced him with a wave of the hand.

"What's your answer, Mr. Chen?" said Carson.

"Give us ten minutes to think it over," Doc replied.

"You've got five," said Carson. He then moved away from the stairs and disappeared into the hallway.

Rock turned around and glanced at the group. "Well, if anyone's got any bright ideas, now's the time to share," he said. His gaze then lingered on Lucielle, "You! Got anything, yet?"

"Me?" the girl asked, a little taken aback.

"You're the big shot analyst, aren't you? I thought you were supposed to come up with all kinds of strategies."

"You're oversimplifying it," she said. "It doesn't work that way."

The giant rolled his eyes. "Yeah, figures."

"Give her a break, will you," said the redhead mercenary. "She's only eleven."

"And a half," Rock corrected as he stared at the girl.

"Take it easy, big guy," said Soran. "You're not helping."

Rock immediately turned his attention to the young man. "Speaking of which … you're supposed to be some kind of big shot too. Well, isn't it time for you to do your thing?"

Soran gave a dubious frown. "And what is *my thing?*"

"I don't know," said the giant. "Go down there and beat the crap out of them or something."

"Are you crazy?" Soran protested. "There's like a dozen of them. And they've got guns. I'll get killed if I go down there. Getting killed is not my thing."

"Keep your voices down," Doc snapped. "We need to come up with a plan. And soon."

Everyone turned silent as they each racked their brain, trying to find a way out of their predicament.

There was now less than three minutes left.

Doc had gone through a number of scenarios in his head, but none of them ended well for his side.

Their situation seemed hopeless.

"Maybe we should try to shoot our way out," said Rock. "I'm sure they're not expecting it."

"No, that wouldn't work," Soran argued. "You said it yourself, they're no amateurs."

"Some of us could sneak out the windows and attack them from outside," Sonar suggested. "We could cover the others and give them a chance to make a run for it."

"No, that wouldn't work either," said Ashrem. "If we split up, it'll only make it easier for them to pick us off one-by-one."

Doc was half-listening to his companions as he continued to think. But then, from the corner of his eye, he saw Lucielle discreetly nod to him. She and the professor had moved to the other end of the room, and she had silently asked the mercenary to join them.

While the others were still busy trying to figure out their next move, Doc furtively went over to the pair and found them arguing in hushed tones.

"You're not seriously suggesting this, are you?" Fournier whispered to the girl.

"I don't think we have a choice," she whispered back.

"It's a terrible idea," the old man insisted.

"What's all this about?" Doc asked, in a similarly low voice.

"It's something Rock said," Lucielle murmured.

Doc rolled his eyes. "Don't pay attention to him. Everyone else tries not to."

"Actually …" the girl said.

"Actually, what?" Doc asked.

"There may be a way to solve our problem," Lucielle declared, still whispering. "But it's extremely dangerous."

Doc's eyebrows arched in surprise. "Really? Let's hear it then."

By then, the rest of the group had noticed the trio's odd behavior and had started to get curious about their mysterious conversation.

"What's going on?" Rock asked.

"Yeah, what's with all the secrecy?" said Soran.

"You have one minute," Carson shouted from below.

Doc Chen turned to Lucielle and said, "All right, we're out of time. We'll go with your plan. What do you need?"

"Just a moment," she said.

The young girl walked over to Rock and waved for him to lean down. She then whispered something in his ear as the others looked on with increasing curiosity.

All of a sudden, the giant jerked back away from her. "Is this a joke? Because we don't—"

"It's not a joke," she interrupted. "There's no time to explain."

"What's going on, Luce?" Ashrem asked.

"She has an idea on how to get us out of this mess," said Doc.

"She does? Right on!" Sonar exclaimed.

Marie had not said a word since Carson's ultimatum. Even though she still had no idea what was going on, one thing, at least, was clear: as far as the men downstairs were concerned, she was in the same boat as that strange group. Therefore, in the immediate future, her only option was to work with them to try to make it out of the house. Which was why she could no longer remain silent. "You want to do what the child says?" she asked the others, in a tone that emphasized the absurdity of their decision.

"Don't worry," Soran told her. "Lucielle knows what she's doing."

"Can I get everyone's attention please," said the analyst as she moved closer to the edge of the stairs.

The rest of the group assembled around her.

She gazed up at them and said, "The plan's actually quite simple. But it's very risky. And it's going to seem rather strange to some of you. Even so, I need everyone to remain calm and do exactly as instructed."

Rock was fidgeting. And he kept casting strange glances at Lucielle. "Are you sure about this?" he finally blurted out.

"Will you please just do what she tells you," Doc told the giant.

Rock sighed in irritation and said, "Fine." Then, without warning, he turned to Soran and grabbed him by the collar. "Sorry, buddy."

"Huh?" The young man stared at the giant in utter bewilderment. But before he could say anything, Rock tossed him over the staircase railings.

"Whoaaa!" Soran shouted as he fell down to the ground floor.

The others looked on, stupefied.

They all heard a thumping sound as Soran hit the ground. And then, nothing.

"What the hell was that?" Doc shouted at his comrade.

"Now, hold on a second," Rock shouted back. "You're the one who told me to do what she said," he added, pointing at the girl with silver hair.

All eyes turned to Lucielle.

Seeing all those accusatory stares converge on her, the youngster became defensive. "What? I told you the plan was simple."

Ashrem moved closer to his sister, and said in a calm voice, "That's a big gamble, Luce. And even if it works, we'll still be in danger."

"Yeah, I said that too," she told him, in a belligerent tone.

At that moment, muffled voices rose from the living room downstairs, where Carson's men had taken Soran. The words themselves weren't clear, but it sounded like threats were being made. Carson was probably asking the young man why he had been delivered to him in such a fashion. And although he couldn't be sure whether this had been an incredibly sloppy mistake, or part of some strange ploy, it was clear that Leicester's associate was starting to lose patience.

"That doesn't sound good," said Rock as they all stood still and listened.

"Hey, at least they're talking," said Sonar.

Doc stared at Lucielle with searching eyes. "You don't really expect your brother to talk us out of this, do you?"

"No, I don't," she replied, with a worried frown on her face.

The voices downstairs had gotten louder.

Then, all of a sudden, nothing. There was complete silence.

But the silence only lasted an instant. It was soon followed by an eruption of screams and gunfire.

"Argh, crap!" Rock exclaimed. "I knew I shouldn't have listened to you."

As the giant headed for the stairs, closely followed by his two comrades, Ashrem stood in their path.

"You shouldn't go down there, right now," said the young man.

"What? We have to go help him," said Rock.

"Don't!" said Fournier. "All of you, stay where you are!"

"Please, trust us on this," said Lucielle.

Meanwhile, it sounded like a war was raging on beneath their feet.

At that point, it occurred to Doc Chen the fighting had been going on for nearly half-a-minute. *Is he really holding up against Carson's entire squad all by himself?* He wondered. He gazed at Ashrem, Lucielle, and the professor in turn. All three had the same troubled look on their faces. But oddly enough, they didn't appear to be focused on what was happening downstairs. They were staring vacantly into space, as if pondering some other matter.

Doc noticed his two comrades casting pressing glances at him. "We'll wait," he told them.

"This is insane!" Marie exclaimed. "Are you really going to let your friend get killed without lifting a finger?"

"He's not our friend," Ashrem told her. "He's our brother. And he'll be fine."

"If you actually believe that, then why do the three of you look so worried?" Marie countered as she cast an eye over the two siblings and the professor.

"We're not worried about our brother," said Lucielle. She approached the staircase banister and cautiously peered below. "We're worried about the rest of us. Especially, about the four of you."

Chapter 11 – Stay Away

Before long, the lower half of the house had turned completely silent. Although, sporadic shots and loud voices could still be heard in the driveway outside.

Ashrem decided to head over to his room to take a peek through the window.

But as soon as the young man moved away from the stairs, Rock shouted, "This is nuts!"

The giant had had enough. He'd held out as long as he could, but his fiery temperament simply would not allow him to wait around any longer, safely away from the action, while a member of his group was in peril. Especially since he was the one who had put him in that situation. Ignoring the others' repeated warnings, he rushed down the stairs and ran out the door.

His redheaded companion followed right on his heels.

"What are you doing?" Lucielle shrieked.

But they were already gone.

The young girl shot an alarmed look at both Ashrem and the professor, and then darted down the stairs after the two mercenaries.

"Luce, wait!" Ashrem shouted. But as he moved to intercept her, he felt a strong jolt of pain inside his chest. His body was reminding him that it was not yet ready to handle the strain of such a surge of energy. He let out a faint groan as he leaned on the door frame and placed his hand over his chest.

"You guys wait here," said Doc. "We'll come back for you when it's safe."

Left with no other choice but to back up his comrades, the third mercenary hurried down steps as well.

Fournier turned to Ashrem and said, "We have to get to him before they do."

"I know," said Ashrem. "I'll go." As he crossed the lounge, the young man glanced at the detective and said, "Please stay here with the professor." He then made his way down the stairs.

Unlike the others, Marie had no problem heeding that advice. She was wrapped up in so much confusion that she could barely move a muscle. And even if she could, she wouldn't have known what to do. At that point, she was seriously questioning the sanity of not only the man she had sought out, but also that of the people around him. *They're insane. They're all insane,* she told herself.

When Ashrem reached the base of the staircase, he heard a sound come from the living room. He approached quietly and peeked through the doorway.

Doc Chen stood in the middle of the room, looking around.

"Hulin?" Ashrem called.

But Doc didn't answer. He didn't even glance back as his name was called.

Ashrem understood right away why he had received no acknowledgment from the mercenary. It wasn't hard for the young man to guess what had induced this state of stunned silence. He had seen it before. And when he stepped through the doorway and scanned the living room, the gruesome scene before him more or less matched what he had expected.

The sofas, tables, chairs, and shelves were smashed or turned upside down. And splashes of blood covered the furniture, the floor, the walls, and even the ceiling.

Ashrem counted nine bodies. And some of them had frozen ghastly expressions. It was as though the fear they had felt right before the end had been imprinted on their faces.

Four of the men had been shot.

Those were the lucky ones.

Another three had had their throats crushed, squeezed like plastic straws. They would have either suffocated or choked on their own blood.

One of the bodies was lying face down next to the fireplace, still clutching at his gun. He had been impaled with the fire iron.

The last victim had been thrown into the field at the back, about fifty feet past the glass bay windows. His body lay on the grass, contorted in a disturbingly unnatural shape.

Finally breaking free of his stupor, Doc turned to Ashrem. "Your brother did this?" he asked, waving at the grisly spectacle.

"Yes."

"How?"

"I'll explain later," said Ashrem. "For now, I need you to help me bring the others back."

Doc stared at him for a moment and then nodded. "Let's go."

The two men exited the house and stepped out onto the driveway. It was completely quiet now. There was no trace of Carson and his remaining men, nor of Lucielle and the two mercenaries. Soran too was nowhere to be seen.

With his gun in hand at the ready, Doc made a wide circle around the professor's car, which they had parked in front of the house to make room for the van inside the shed. Once he saw that no one was hiding behind the vehicle, he headed for the gate. He wanted to check the narrow road that passed in front of the house.

Ashrem stopped him. "No, it's better if you stay close. Besides, the bushes on the other side of the road are too high, you'll have little visibility. It's too dangerous."

"I don't think we need to worry about Carson and his men anymore," said Doc. "At least, not for now."

"I know," Ashrem replied as he turned and gazed up at the roof.

At that moment, Lucielle emerged from the shed, accompanied by Rock and Sonar.

Ashrem let out a deep sigh. He was relieved to see the three of them unharmed.

Still on high alert, Doc nodded at his two comrades.

The redhead shook his head in response to signal they had found no one inside.

But then, all heads promptly turned towards the gate when they heard a creaking sound.

It was Soran.

The young man pushed open the small wooden gate and calmly walked in. His demeanor was that of someone returning from an afternoon stroll in the countryside. But his blue t-shirt, black jeans, and black shoes were splattered with red patches. And drops of blood were still dripping from his fingertips.

"Hey, look who's still alive and in one piece!" Rock cheered as he and Sonar jogged to meet the young man.

"No, stay away from him!" Lucielle shouted. "That's not Soran. That's Myrvan!"

Rock stopped and glanced back at her with a quizzical expression. "What the hell's a Myrvan?" he asked.

While his head was turned, the giant received a violent kick to the midsection. He was sent flying over twenty feet through the air before he crashed into Professor Fournier's car, shattering the rear windshield and making a big dent on the trunk.

"What are you doing?" Sonar exclaimed as he stared uncomprehendingly at the young man.

Soran glared at him. Then, he grabbed the redhead by the collar and hurled him at the shed.

The mercenary impacted the shed wall with a heavy thump and knocked his head hard against a wooden panel. He then dropped like a lump of metal, and remained on the ground, motionless.

Doc immediately leveled his weapon at Soran, though he still didn't understand why the young man had attacked his two comrades. But then he heard Rock moan, and mechanically turned his head to check on him. The giant had rolled off the car, but was still too dizzy to get back to his feet.

"Watch out!" Ashrem shouted.

Doc promptly whipped his head back towards the front. He had only looked away for an instant, and yet, to his utter amazement, Soran was now less than six feet away from him. He shuddered. *How is he so close already?*

In the face of the imminent danger, Doc Chen's instinct and experience as a soldier took over. He fired two shots in rapid succession.

All he hit was dirt and dust.

Soran had already dodged to the side before the first bullet had left its chamber. The young man slapped the gun away from Doc and readied himself to strike him.

Fortunately, Ashrem intervened and intercepted the punch rocketing towards Doc's face, stopping it inches away from its target.

Without a word, Soran glared at his brother and launched a devastating sidekick to his ribcage.

Ashrem was propelled backwards, and rolled on the ground over several feet.

Doc was now alone, unarmed, and face-to-face with Soran.

But was it even him?

As the mercenary stared at his terrifying opponent, he realized nothing about the young man seemed familiar. His body posture, his facial expressions, his eyes … Doc didn't recognize any of it.

But that was a purely academic consideration. The fact remained, the person standing before him was extremely dangerous and clearly intent on hurting him.

Doc was fully aware of the peril he faced. He knew he wouldn't last more than a few seconds in a hand-to-hand confrontation against his genetically engineered opponent. He took a quick step back, trying to keep his distance. But Soran lunged after him.

Then, all of a sudden, the young man jumped back in the opposite direction.

A shot had been fired from above and the bullet had impacted the ground at the exact spot where Soran had been standing a split-second earlier. Somehow, he had sensed the danger and had moved away in time to avoid getting hit.

Doc turned his head around and looked up.

He saw Marie and the professor standing at the window in Ashrem's room. The detective was holding her gun with both hands and was aiming it down at the driveway.

Marie was stunned. She couldn't believe how quickly Soran had reacted. She couldn't understand how he had been able to change direction with such speed and agility. *How can a person move like that?* she asked herself.

Despite her bewilderment, the detective adjusted her aim and prepared to fire again.

But Soran wouldn't give her the chance.

The young man pounced on Doc and lifted him up by the torso, using him as a shield to obstruct the detective's line of fire.

Doc barely had time to grasp what was happening as his attacker spun him around once, and then launched him at the second-floor window.

Marie froze in shock as she stared, gaping mouth, at the human projectile flying straight at her.

Professor Fournier, however, was not the least bit surprised. Which meant that he still had his wits about him. He tackled the detective down to the floor just as Doc came crashing through the window, thereby minimizing the damage resulting from their collision.

By then, Rock had shaken off the dizziness and was ready to join the action.

Unfortunately, Soran was already close to him.

No sooner had the giant returned to his feet than he felt a strong pinch around his neck. Soran had gripped him by the throat and was applying a tremendous amount of pressure.

The giant immediately experienced difficulty breathing.

He contracted the thick muscles in his neck to buy himself some time. No more than an extra second or two, but that was all he needed. Rock's training and experience had taught him how to get out of various holds and locks. He swung both of his forearms hard against the outstretched arm, simultaneously hitting his opponent's wrist and elbow from opposite directions.

Nothing happened.

He tried again … still no result.

The giant shuddered as he realized he was literally a breath away from having his windpipes crushed.

Luckily, Ashrem returned in time to save him.

The young man pulled Soran back and tried to bring him to the ground in an attempt to subdue him, if only for a short time.

The two brothers grappled for a while as they continued to move away. But Ashrem was too weakened by his injuries to carry his plan to fruition.

Soran planted his feet firmly on the ground and broke free of his brother's hold. He then swung his arm and delivered a powerful backhanded fist to the side of Ashrem's head, sending him swirling through the air.

Having had time to catch his breath, Rock seized the opportunity to reach for the gun tucked behind him inside his belt.

For the second time, Soran somehow sensed a danger from his blind spot. He spun around and glared at the giant.

Without hesitation, Rock fired three times as the young man closed in on him at an alarming speed.

But Soran proved to be a most disobliging target. He rushed forward, half stood up and zig-zagging on his toes, like some wild beast charging down its prey. His movements were so quick and so irregular that it was extremely difficult to anticipate his next position. As a result, the first two bullets missed their mark. But the third one lodged itself into the young man's midsection.

Instead of slowing him down, the gunshot wound only seemed to enrage Soran further. He pounced on the giant and grabbed him by the wrists.

In an attempt to break free, Rock abruptly pulled his arms back.

It was no use.

"What the hell are you doing?" he shouted, trying to bring Soran back to his senses.

That too failed.

The giant grimaced with pain as he felt his arms twist to the point where he thought his ligaments would snap.

He had to do something. Now.

Rock had always been a firm believer that the best kind of defense was a good offense. He gritted his teeth and lunged headfirst at his opponent.

Their heads collided violently.

Though it was unorthodox, the mercenary's desperate attack had yielded the desired result. Soran had let go. But the collision had left the giant stunned, both literally and figuratively. He felt like he had just clashed heads with a ram.

Wobbly from the shock, Rock staggered back and fell on his backside. But it wasn't until he heard the click of the hammer being cocked that he realized his weapon was no longer in his hand.

He looked up, and saw the muzzle of his own gun pointed down at him.

There was nothing else he could try, no more tricks up his sleeve. This was it.

The giant had all but resigned himself to his fate, when, out of nowhere, Lucielle jumped between the two men and spread her arms to make her body as big as possible.

"No, don't!" She pleaded to her brother. "You have to stop. Please."

Soran stared impassively at the young girl. It was almost like he didn't know who she was. Then, his brow twitched and his head tilted to the side as he continued to stare at her.

What followed next was so bizarre that the giant froze in astonishment as he looked on.

"Luce ..." Soran said in a low voice.

The young man's hands began to shake. Only a little, at first. But as the seconds passed, the shaking grew more intense. Eventually, the gun fell to the ground because Soran could no longer hold it. He closed his eyes and pressed his hands against his temples as he moaned and staggered backwards.

He seemed to be in pain. A lot of it.

He tottered awkwardly for a while longer, and then, suddenly, collapsed on the ground, unconscious.

Chapter 12 – Monsters

"Phew!" Lucielle sighed in relief. "It's over."

"It's over? What's over?" Rock demanded as he got back up. "What the hell just happened?"

"Is everyone all right?" Doc called out as he ran out of the house, followed by Marie and the professor.

"We're fine," said Rock.

"And Sonar?" Doc asked.

Everyone turned towards the shed.

The redheaded mercenary was half stood up, with his hands on his knees. When he raised his head and met the others' worried gazes, he forced a weak smile and gave a thumbs-up to signal he was OK.

"He'll be fine," said Rock. "He just banged his head a little, that's all. I'm more interested in what happened with this one," he added as he pointed at Soran who was lying on the ground, asleep.

Meanwhile, Fournier had gone over to Ashrem to help him up. "Are you all right, son?"

"Yes," the young man replied. "I'm just glad it's over."

Upon hearing Ashrem repeat the same phrase as Lucielle, without once again offering any kind of explanation, Rock grew even more incensed. "All right, that's it!" he grumbled. "The next one who says that … I'm gonna shoot him. Or her," he added, looking at the young girl.

"I'm afraid the explanation will have to wait," said Fournier. "Might I suggest we relocate first?"

"Yes," said the young analyst. "This place obviously isn't safe anymore."

"I agree," said Doc. "Our first priority should be to get away from here. There'll be plenty of time to talk later."

Rock grunted in frustration, but made no objections.

"Hmm, looks like the professor's car is toast," Lucielle said in a nonchalant voice. "It's a good thing we still have the van." She then turned to the blond woman. "I assume you have a car somewhere nearby?"

"Yes," Marie replied in a wary voice.

"Good, so what will it be?"

The detective gave a blank look.

"What will it be?" the youngster repeated. "Will you go off on your own, or are you coming with us?"

Fournier could hardly believe his ears. "What are you saying, Luce? Of course she's leaving. She should return to Berlin at once, and forget all about this."

"I don't know, professor," said Lucielle. "It couldn't have been easy for her to track you all the way here. I doubt she'll quietly go back home just because you're asking so nicely. Besides, there's a high probability Carson followed her here. At the very least, he saw her come into the house. Which means it's only a matter of time before Andrew finds out who she is." The silver-haired girl paused and squinted into space. "That's assuming he doesn't already know. He's very sneaky that one."

Marie tilted her head. "Andrew?"

"Yes, Andrew Leicester," Lucielle replied. "The men who attacked us work for him."

"I think the kid might be right," Doc said to the detective. "If they know about you, you're probably safer with us for the time being."

The detective paused as she considered their offer.

On the one hand, this was her best chance to uncover the truth about Professor Karpov's past, and to find out the motive behind his murder. After what she had just witnessed, Marie had no doubt this odd bunch was connected to the group she had encountered on the previous night—which included Professor Karpov's killer.

But on the other hand, she didn't know these people. Was it wise to tag along with a group of strangers? And not just any strangers, these guys were clearly involved in something dangerous. Not ten minutes after she had met them, heavily armed men had shown up out of nowhere and had started shooting at everyone. And in response, this group had inexplicably opted to serve up one of their own to the attackers by tossing him over a second-floor banister. *Sure, that made a lot of sense*, Marie joked to herself.

Then, she thought about how Soran had turned on them with a murderous rage. She went over his actions in her head. How could he have done the things he had done? How could anyone? She remembered the blond man with the knives, and how strong he too was. She was overwhelmed by it all. It almost felt like none of it was real. Like it was some kind of dream. And why on earth was the child making all the decisions?

Marie closed her eyes as she tried to collect herself. But she was quickly jolted out of her contemplation by the sound of a harsh clap.

"Hey, Lady! We don't have all day here," Rock complained.

Marie glanced at the old man. Professor Karpov had told her that Jerome Fournier was his best friend. So maybe she could trust him, even though he seemed hell-bent on sending her away. In fact, it was his reluctance to talk to her which convinced Marie she could trust him. He reminded her of Professor Karpov, and of how he had always refused to tell her anything about his past because he wanted to protect her. Clearly, that was also Professor Fournier's intention. He was trying to keep her away from danger because he knew that's what his friend would have wanted.

"Sorry," she finally said. "Yes, I would like to go with you."

"It's settled, then," Doc declared.

Lucielle walked over to Rock and tugged on his sleeve.

"What do you want, kid?"

She pointed at Soran who was still peacefully sleeping on the ground next to them and asked, "Would you mind carrying him to the van?"

The giant froze for a long time as he tried to decide whether the girl was being serious or not. He glanced at Soran, and then back at her. "Are you kidding me? Is she kidding me?" He asked again, this time turning to Ashrem and the professor.

The two men stared back at him but said nothing.

When Rock realized their silence was meant as a tacit approval of the young girl's suggestion, he snapped. "Are you all freaking nuts?"

True to his nickname, Sonar had heard the entire exchange from the shed. He jogged over to the group and said, "Whoa! You guys aren't serious, are you?"

"We can't leave him here," Ashrem said.

"Oh, yes we can," Rock replied.

"Why in the world would we do that?" Lucielle asked in an angered voice.

"Hmm … let me think," said the giant as he placed his finger over his mouth as though he was pondering his answer. "How about because he just went all *postal* on us?" he barked at the young girl.

"We told you to wait upstairs," Lucielle retorted. "In any case, it's OK. He's fine, now."

"Is he? Well, if you say so … I guess that clears everything up, doesn't it?" Rock said in an overly sarcastic tone.

"No, she's right," said Fournier. "I'm quite certain the … episode is over."

"Episode?" Sonar echoed. "Really? Is that what we're calling this?"

"What if he's still lying here when Andrew's men return?" Lucielle challenged.

"Hey, clearly your brother is far scarier than Carson and his goons," the giant countered.

"That wasn't Soran. That was Myrvan," said Lucielle, her tone growing more impatient.

Doc turned to her, intrigued. "You said the same thing earlier. What does it mean?"

Fournier sighed. There was no time to get into details, but he realized he would have to give the mercenaries something if they were going to agree to bring the young man along with them. "Soran suffers from a kind of dissociative identity disorder," he said. "Or MPD, if you prefer."

"Multiple personality disorder?" Doc checked.

"Correct," said Fournier. "Soran's the one you've been interacting with this entire time. And now, you've met his alter ego: Myrvan."

Rock threw his arms up in the air. "Give me a break, man. Alter ego? What is he? A villain?"

"If that's the case," Doc said. "Can you guys honestly tell us you know which one he'll be when he wakes up?"

"Yes," Fournier replied without hesitation. "But it would take time to explain. More time than we currently have."

"And where do you suggest we take him?" Sonar asked.

"There's a place. In Paris," said the old man.

Doc thought about it for a while and then finally said, "Very well. We'll call Nate from the road and tell him to meet us there." He then looked at Soran. "We'll take him with us. I'll patch up his wound. Rock, try to find something to tie him up with. And make sure it's strong enough to hold him."

"Fine," the giant replied, visibly not happy about the decision.

"Don't worry," said Lucielle. "He probably won't wake up for a while."

Rock grunted as he headed to the shed. He had spotted a chain and a heavy rope earlier when they had looked inside.

"Where's your car?" Doc asked Marie.

She stared at him briefly before she answered. "Fifty meters or so down the road."

"OK. I'll ride with you when we're ready to leave."

Marie gave a surprised look. "You want to come with me?"

"Sure," Doc replied. "Why cram everyone into the van when there's room inside your car? Besides, that way you'll have someone to keep you company."

Marie knew the real reason for Doc's suggestion was that he didn't trust her. He didn't want to leave her alone to follow them in her car. Instead, he preferred to keep an eye on her. But she understood. It was a reasonable precaution to take, considering they had just met. "Of course," she said.

A short time later, the professor's van rolled out of his property and turned onto the small road passing in front of it. Professor Fournier was driving, with the redhead mercenary riding in front with him. Rock, Ashrem, and Lucielle were seated at the back, along with Soran, whose hands and feet had been tightly wrapped in rope and chains.

Following close behind the van, Marie and Doc Chen rode in the detective's car.

The group had only travelled about a hundred feet when they spotted two figures on the side of the road.

The vehicles stopped.

The bodies of two of Carson's men were lying on the side of the road.

"I guess that explains what he was doing outside," said Doc.

Marie turned to him, perplexed. "Your friend did this?"

Doc nodded.

The detective gazed back at the bodies and said, "But if they're here, doesn't that mean …"

"Yeah, they were trying to run away," said Doc.

"And he chased them all the way here? … to kill them?"

Marie felt a shiver run up her spine. She had seen the horrifying scene inside the living room. But finding those two corpses here was almost as disturbing.

Like the mercenaries, the detective had had a hard time believing that Soran could have decimated Carson's entire squad all by himself, and in such a short period of time. Normally, she would have discarded the idea as being impossible. But the word *impossible* had surfaced far too often in the past twenty-four hours.

She knew Soran had done it. She just didn't understand how.

Upon witnessing the carnage inside the living room, Marie had told herself that such savage brutality could only have been the result of a strong instinct for survival. Soran had been so afraid for his life that he had turned excessively violent and aggressive.

That was her theory.

That theory, however, could not account for the two bodies in front of her now. The fact that Soran had chased those men so far outside the property, like a predator refusing to let his prey escape. That fact left her with only one possible conclusion. It was the same conclusion she had reached in regards to Professor Karpov's self-professed murderer.

They were both monsters.

Without realizing it, she had entered a world bound by different rules, woven with different threads. A world of incredibly smart and wise men, like Professor Karpov. A world of giants, and of mysterious children. But also, a world of monsters.

Chapter 13 – Refuge

It was a little after 11 p.m. when Professor Fournier drove his white van past the metallic gates of a quiet residential building near the *Porte d' Auteuil* in Paris. He proceeded down the ramp and stopped in front of the garage door. Once the gates closed behind him, the garage door crawled up along the ceiling with a heavy rumble, and opened into an underground parking lot.

The professor drove his van inside and parked into one of the slots on the lower levels.

"We're here," he said as he turned off the engine.

"Good," said Sonar. "I don't know why, but the drive to Paris felt even longer this time."

His comment was met with complete silence.

It hadn't been a particularly long trip, but it had been a noticeably quiet one. The events at the professor's house had left the group in a sombre mood. And with the exception of Lucielle and the old man, everyone had suffered one or more injuries—some minor, but others more severe.

"We should hurry," said Fournier as he opened the driver-side door. "I'd rather we didn't come across any of the other residents. There's rarely anyone going in or out of the building at this hour, but you never know."

Sonar nodded. He grabbed his gear and exited from the front passenger side.

Ashrem opened the rear doors and stepped out, followed by Lucielle and Rock. The giant then turned around and leaned inside the vehicle. He dragged Soran by the feet and flung him over his right shoulder. The young man was still sound asleep.

"Can you get my gear?" Rock said to Ashrem as he nodded towards his black sports bag.

"Sure," Ashrem replied. He leaned inside and grabbed the bag by its straps. But as soon as he started pulling it, he let go and grunted in pain—he was in an even worse shape since the fight with his brother.

"Never mind," said Rock. "I'll take it." He stretched out his left arm and retrieved the bag while keeping Soran balanced on his right shoulder.

Lucielle then slammed the rear doors shut.

Fournier led the group to a small door, which opened into a dimly lit corridor stretching about forty feet to the main elevator. And immediately to their right was a service elevator and the staircase door.

"Let's use the service elevator," Fournier suggested. "We'll have less chance of running into someone."

"How many people live here?" Rock asked.

"This is the main building," the old man explained. "There are only two apartments per floor, so not that many people. The building across the courtyard has a lot more occupants, though there typically wouldn't be any reason for them to use the elevators on this side at this time of night."

The group rode the service elevator to the seventh floor and exited onto a staircase landing with two doors opposite each other.

Fournier took out a four-sided key and opened the door on the left.

They entered into a large fully-fitted kitchen with dark green tiles, big windows, and a rectangular wooden table. They proceeded beyond the kitchen and into a large reception area. Behind them was the main entrance door, and in front, at the end of the reception hall, were two smaller doors. Fournier told them that each one led to a different corridor with a separate set of bedrooms and bathrooms.

The double door to their right opened onto a spacious living room connected to a dining room.

The décor inside the living room was European classic: a marble fireplace, polished wooden flooring, candle-shaped lightbulbs, and a chandelier hanging from the ceiling. The living room was fitted with a large flat-screen TV, a coffee table, and two sofas—a three-seater and a two-seater—with light-green upholstery embroidered with dark green motifs matching the curtains.

The side of the living room facing the streets consisted of floor-to-ceiling windows with security roller blinds. And the windows granted access to a balcony overlooking a small park across the road.

"Hey Pops, how big is this place?" Sonar asked.

Fournier scratched his head. "I'm not sure. It's quite big, though."

Having spent so much of her young life hidden away in one isolated house or another, Lucielle always relished the opportunity to explore new surroundings. She scurried across the entrance hall like a little mouse and disappeared behind the right-hand side hallway door.

"Where's she going?" Rock asked after the young girl had whizzed out of sight.

The professor smiled. "Don't mind her, she—"

He was interrupted by a soft double knock.

They all paused as the old man walked to the entrance door and peered through the peephole.

"It's them," said Fournier. He opened the door and let Doc and Marie in. "I trust you didn't have too much trouble finding a parking spot?" he asked them.

"No," Marie replied. "We found one a block down the road."

Doc Chen dropped his bag on the floor, next to the coat holder, and then turned to his comrades. "Did you clear the apartment?"

"No, not yet," Sonar replied.

Lucielle suddenly came out of the hallway and ran back to the group, literally stopping right under Fournier's nose. "What is this place, Professor?"

"Well, technically speaking, it belongs to you," he said. "To you and your siblings."

"What do you mean?" she asked.

"This was one of Adam's hideouts after he had escaped from the Arc. I imagine the reason he chose such a big place was that he meant for his children to use it someday. Possibly as a temporary refuge, like he had done."

"A hideout? In the middle of the city?" Sonar exclaimed.

"You must remember," said Fournier. "Due to the sensitive nature of our project, Leicester and his associates couldn't involve the police in their search for us. They couldn't exactly start an international manhunt. They had to rely on their own people, and remain very discreet about it. Besides, I'm sure they had fully expected us to have booked tickets to some far-off destination the minute we went missing. A big city is the last place they would have looked. I chose an isolated area because I actually like the countryside, and I enjoy taking long walks on the beach. But Alek hid in Berlin for years without anyone finding out."

"That didn't work out too well for him in the end, though," Rock pointed out.

Fournier didn't respond. But both he and Lucielle mechanically shot uneasy glances at Marie.

"In any case," the old man said, eager to change the subject. "I guess we need to wait for Arianne and Mr. Kincade to arrive before doing anything else. In the meantime, please make yourselves at home."

"Where should I put sleeping beauty, here?" Rock said as he padded Soran on the back.

"Shouldn't he have woken up by now?" Doc asked.

"Normally, yes," Fournier replied. "But, typically when Myrvan emerges, he stays for hours, or even days. The change between the two personalities is never without … complications. His mind needs time to adjust to it. However, in this case, due to Lucielle's intervention, Myrvan's appearance was very brief. It only lasted a few minutes. That quick back-and-forth probably put a big strain on his psyche. And on top of that, his actions must have also taken quite a toll on his body as well." Fournier paused and gazed at Soran with tender eyes. "I'm sure he'll be up soon. Let's put him in one of the bedrooms. Please, follow me," he told Rock as he headed towards the back of the apartment.

"I think you can untie him now," said Lucielle as the two men walked away.

"Yeah, that's not gonna happen," Rock said, without looking back.

Doc and Sonar also left the living room to perform a thorough sweep of the apartment and to find an area to settle in, leaving Lucielle alone with the detective.

The young girl dug into her purple-striped bag and fished out her doll and a mini hairbrush. Then, she went to take a seat on the large sofa and began brushing the doll's long dark hair.

Marie watched her for a moment.

Lucielle took great care in handling her doll. Each stroke of her brush was soft and deliberate, as though she was holding a real baby. And all the while, she was humming. She looked like she didn't have a care in the world.

Marie sat next to the youngster and asked, "What's her name?"

Lucielle gave the blond woman a strange look and said, "She doesn't have a name. She's just a doll."

The detective was thrown a little off-balance by Lucielle's detached response. It wasn't at all what she had expected. *Such a curious child*, she thought.

Once again, Marie found herself wondering how this adolescent girl had ended up with this strange group. But even though she was truly curious about Lucielle and about her place in all of this, the questions that burned brightest inside the detective's mind extended far beyond the child's involvement. She still had no idea what was going on. She had attempted to get some answers from Doc Chen during their long drive to Paris, but he had turned out to be a frustratingly tight-lipped traveling companion.

"Do you mind if I ask you some questions?" the detective asked.

"No, go ahead," Lucielle replied as she resumed her meticulous activity.

"I heard one of them say that you were eleven years old. Is that right?"

"Eleven and a half," the girl said, almost sounding like she was boasting about the number.

"Where are your parents?"

"I had a father. Adam. But he's dead now," the young girl said in a stoic tone.

Although she recalled Professor Karpov mentioning that name, Marie cringed in embarrassment for bringing up the subject. "I'm so sorry," she said.

"It's OK," Lucielle told her. "It happened a few years ago."

"And your mother?"

"I don't have a mother," the girl nonchalantly replied.

Marie bit her lower lip. She felt stupid and insensitive for putting her foot in her mouth like that again. "I'm really, truly sorry," she apologized.

Lucielle gazed up at the blond woman. Realizing the detective had misunderstood her statement, the young girl shook her head and said, "It's not what you think. I meant I *never* had a mother."

Marie gave her a puzzled frown. What did she mean? Had she been adopted? Unsure what to make of the girl's remark, she decided it was best to change the subject altogether.

"Who are these people we're waiting for?" the detective asked.

"My sister, Arianne, and Jonathan Kincade. He's their leader," Lucielle explained.

"Leader?"

"Yeah. That huge guy and his two friends. They used to be in the army. But now they work as mercenaries. As in, they fight for money. But they're not bad people. They're helping us."

"Helping you with what?"

"My father hid something before he died," said Lucielle. "Something very important, and probably very dangerous. We're trying to find it before others do."

Marie pointed towards the back of the apartment. "What about the man tied up in there?"

"He's my brother, Soran. He's not a bad person either. Really. He just has some personality issues."

"How was he able to do all of that? It's not possible. And the other night … the blond man with the knives … he did some inexplicable things too."

Lucielle rolled her eyes. "Oh, that one's also my brother, Johann. Sorry about him."

The young girl put the doll down on her laps and said, "Hmm, I suppose there's no point in keeping the truth from you after everything you've seen. Perhaps I'd better start from the beginning."

Chapter 14 – Fractures

Damien entered an apartment in the fifth *arrondissement* [district] in Paris and locked the door behind him. He then proceeded to the living room and found Kadyna and Johann comfortably installed on a beige corner-sofa. She was flipping through the pages of a fashion magazine with dull indifference, while he watched a documentary on TV about lions in the African savanna.

When Damien walked in, Kadyna folded her magazine and turned her head, but Johann continued to watch his program as though he hadn't noticed.

"Still no sign of Mitsuki?" Damien asked.

"Not yet," Kadyna replied.

"What happened?"

"It's like I told you over the phone," Kadyna said. "She created the diversion as planned, but she never showed up at the rendezvous point. I think there's a high probability she ran into Jenkins on her way to meet with us."

"A very high probability," Johann commented, his eyes still glued to the screen. "But it's also possible she decided to take off."

"Shut up, you buffoon!" Kadyna snapped. "Just keep watching your stupid television."

Johann scoffed. "Come on, sis. You know as well as I do that if she was going to ditch us, this would have been the perfect time to do it. None of us ever knows what she's really thinking. Well, maybe except for Darius. But half the time, I have no idea what he's thinking, either."

"Where is he?" Damien asked.

"When Mitsu didn't show, Darius went to look for her," Kadyna explained. "Apparently, there was a horde of police officers and a few of Jenkins' guys loitering near the site of some car accident. Darius said there were signs of a battle, but he didn't see Mitsu there. So, he grabbed one of Jenkins' goons and brought him here with us." Kadyna nodded towards the narrow hallway behind the sofa. "He's in his room, right now, *talking* to the guy."

"And Renard?" Damien asked.

"She's in my bedroom," Kadyna replied. "We had a little talk with her too. As expected, she doesn't know quite as much as Leicester or Schaffer, but she wasn't completely useless. She shared one or two pieces of information which I'm sure you'll find interesting."

"Good," said Damien. "But we'll deal with her later. For now, we still need to find out what happened to Mitsuki."

"Jenkins took her," said Darius as he walked out of his room at the end of the hallway. He then closed the door and joined the others.

"How?" Damien asked him.

"According to the man in there, she intervened to help Ashrem and one of the mercenaries after they were caught by Jenkins. The two of them got away, but she ended up getting captured in their stead."

That got Johann's attention. He put down the remote and turned to his brother. "Why would she care what happens to them?"

"Not, *them*," said Darius. "*Him*. I'm sure she only intended to help Ashrem."

"Why?" Johann asked. "He's the one who chose to side against us?"

Darius stared at him briefly but said nothing.

Damien crossed his arms over his chest and frowned as he started thinking aloud. "An emotional reaction? … from Mitsuki of all people."

A mocking smile appeared on Johann's face. "Don't beat yourself up too much. You did get everything else right. Jenkins, Arianne, Renard, the mercenaries, that idiot Thompson, even Luce. You're six for seven. Over eighty-five percent. That's not bad. After all, even you can't predict everything with absolute certainty. You're bound to let one slip by on occasion."

Damien gave him a cold stare.

Johann wisely decided to stop taunting his brother and slowly looked away.

The silver-haired man turned to Darius and studied him briefly. "You want us to put our mission on hold and go look for Mitsuki, don't you?"

"Yes," said Darius. "If she was indeed taken by Jenkins, we all know what they'll do to her."

"We can't afford any delays," said Damien. "Not when we're this close. Arianne's in possession of the necklace. It won't be long before either she, or one of the others, deciphers Adam's message. If we want the data card, we have no choice but to decipher the code before they do. Then, we'll go get our sister."

Darius gave Damien a long, placid stare. Then, he turned around and slowly walked away.

"Where are you going?" Kadyna asked him.

"To get Renard," Darius replied. "I'll require her assistance to find out where they're holding Mitsuki." He went into his sister's bedroom, and came back out seconds later, leading Nathalie Renard by the arm.

"Where are you taking me?" the French diplomat protested.

"Be quiet," Darius calmly told her.

Renard promptly complied.

Darius scared her. He had a discreet, yet intimidating, presence. And his voice always had the same flat intonation. Then there were those eyes. Cold. Dead. However hard she looked, Renard couldn't find the slightest spark of life in them. And every time he looked in her direction, she felt like he was looking past her. Like she wasn't really there. It made her feel completely expendable. Insignificant, even. And it frightened her.

Kadyna jumped off the sofa and stood in Darius' way. "Why are you always so stubborn?" she yelled. "We've already lost Mitsu. Now you want to leave, too? Are you trying to mess up the entire plan? You heard what Damien said. We'll go get her after we find the card."

"I made myself clear from the beginning," said Darius. "My goal has always been to watch over our family. All of us. That's the promise I made to Adam." He turned to Damien and added, "That responsibility should have been yours. But given your nature, it clearly wasn't an option. Therefore, it falls to me. The only reason I sided with you rather than the others, was to make sure we didn't all end up killing one another. In view of our decisive advantage in numbers, I had hoped Arianne and Ashrem would see reason and give up. Especially, since Soran had chosen to stay out of it altogether." Darius shot a sideways glance at Johann and said, "But because of him, Arianne was able to change Soran's mind. A head-on confrontation now would only result in losses on both sides. That's the very scenario I've been trying to avoid." His eyes shifted back to Damien. "Since I cannot convince you to alter your plans, I will alter mine. I will rescue our sister. I only hope all of you are still alive when I return."

Kadyna took another step forward and stood firmly in front of him. "You're not leaving!" she declared.

"And how exactly do you propose to stop me?" Darius calmly asked her.

Kadyna clenched her fists in frustration. But she refused to back down, and continued to stare defiantly at him.

"Let him go," Damien eventually said. "The three of us are more than enough to finish this," he added as he walked past the pair and headed into his room.

Kadyna stepped aside and looked on with anger as Darius walked out of the apartment with Nathalie Renard.

As soon as they were gone, she turned to Johann and berated him. "You! You're always babbling on about some nonsense when nobody cares what you have to say. But of course, the one time it would actually be useful for you to speak up … not a peep."

Johann smiled and shrugged. "What can I say, sis? Here I thought our little family was doing so well. I'm just so distraught. I simply couldn't find the words."

"Just dry up and die, already!" Kadyna said as she sat back on the sofa and returned to her magazine.

Johann grabbed the remote and turned up the volume of his documentary on African lions.

"There, that should do it," said the doctor as he applied the last stitch on his patient's rib.

"Thanks," said Carson as he stood off the examination table.

"Wait. I still need to place a gauze over it."

"I'll be fine," said Carson. "Tell me about my men."

"Ah, yes. They—"

The doctor was interrupted when the door suddenly opened and four agents in dark suits barged into his office.

Ignoring Carson and the doctor, the men carefully inspected every corner of the room, checked inside every closet, and even peeked under the desk. One of them went to the window, opened it, and took a long look outside and up towards the roof. He then closed it and pulled down the blinds.

"All clear," the agent said in his earpiece.

During the men's thorough inspection, the doctor had remained frozen, staring at them round-eyed and mouth gaping. But when his initial shock finally subsided, he cast a nervous glance around and asked, "What's going on?"

"Relax, Doctor," said Carson as he put on his shirt. "They're just making sure the room is secured."

A man appeared in the doorway, surrounded by another four agents. He was wearing a custom-made gray suit, with a red handkerchief folded inside his top-left pocket.

The man in the gray suit calmly walked in, leaving his entourage to stand guard outside. "I'm glad to see you up and about, Mr. Carson," he said.

"Thank you, sir."

Carson turned to the doctor and made the introductions.

"Doctor Khoursy, this is my employer, Mr. Leicester."

Leicester gave a quick nod. "Doctor Khoursy."

Still unsure of what to make of the situation, the doctor's only response came in the form of a silent nod at the stranger.

Leicester turned to his associate and asked, "What happened?"

Carson's expression hardened. "It was bad. Most of my men didn't make it. Only four of us got out, including myself and your man, Stanwell."

"Indeed. I'm glad you were able to retrieve Mark safely. I trust he's well?"

"He's fine. He ran out of there pretty fast when things turned ugly."

Leicester smiled. "Yes, I'm sure he did. And what of your men?"

Carson turned to the man in the white blouse. "The doctor was just about to give me an update on Simmons and Bartlett when you arrived."

Seeing the questioning stares directed at him, Doctor Khoursy shook off his surprise. He stared back at Leicester and asked, "I'm sorry, who are you?"

"Mr. Carson just told you, I'm his employer. Your other two patients are also associates of mine. What's their condition?"

Doctor Khoursy hesitated for a moment, and then gave his report. "Ahem. Well, they've each suffered a number of fractures and have possible concussions, but nothing life-threatening. In time, I expect they'll both make a full recovery."

"Thank you, Doctor," said Leicester.

Doctor Khoursy nodded again. But as the Briton continued to hold him in his gaze, the doctor realized he was being invited to leave. He scowled at the stranger. Not only did he not appreciate being dismissed so offhandedly by this man who wasn't even a patient, but this was actually his office.

The doctor cast another glance around the room. Aside from Leicester, who exhibited a rather pleasant smile, none of the other men present seemed particularly amicable. Without saying another word, he picked up a folder off his desk and left.

Leicester then turned to Carson. "Tell me exactly what happened."

Carson hesitated as he shot quick glances at the agents inside the room.

The British diplomat dismissed his security team with a nod.

Once the agents were gone, Carson gave an account of what had transpired at Professor Fournier's home. "We followed that German detective like you asked. And it paid off. Much sooner than we had expected. She led us straight to a group of fugitives. Most of Kincade's team were also there with them. When we proceeded to surround the house, some of my men were spotted. Having lost the element of surprise, they decided to engage the targets."

Leicester frowned. "Where was Lucielle during all of this?"

"The analyst was inside with the others," Carson replied.

"And your men fired at the house?" said the Briton, the tone of his voice rising slightly.

"When I heard the shot, I immediately ordered my men to stand down. But since the fugitives had been alerted to our presence, we needed to move fast. We knew the analyst was in a room on the upper level, so I instructed my men to limit their fire to the ground floor. We stormed the house and forced them up the stairs. We had them trapped on the second floor, with our backup teams less than half an hour away."

"Did you offer them terms?" Leicester asked.

"I did. I told them that if the fugitives and the professor agreed to come with us, my men and I would leave peacefully."

"How did they respond?"

"In a very peculiar way," said Carson. "They tossed one of their own over the staircase railings, basically handing him over to us. It was a completely unexpected move. At the time, I had no idea who the guy was. But now, I realize he must have been one of the fugitives. The one not in the pictures you gave to me and Kincade."

"Soran," said Leicester.

"Is that his name?" said Carson. "I must admit, I wasn't sure what to think, at first. So we took him to the living room to question him. I don't know if it was an act but he seemed genuinely worried, even frightened. I assumed handing him over was part of some stalling tactic, so I ordered my men to get their stun grenades and prepare for an assault. The guy, Soran, argued against it. One of my men got a bit rough with him, and hit him on the head with the cross of his rifle. Hard."

"Oh … that was a mistake," said Leicester.

"I'd say. My squad was practically wiped out. It was like he changed. The fear was gone. And he became extremely aggressive. I didn't get the impression it was about defending himself or protecting the others anymore. No, this felt more like … instinct. Like he wanted to kill us simply because we were there. I'm not sure how to explain it."

Carson spoke in a low and measured voice, but Leicester could tell he had been shaken by the experience.

"I've seen Patrick do some incredible things over the years," Carson continued. "But this … this was different. My men are professionals. But that guy cut through them like they were nothing more than target practice. If this is what we're up against, I suggest we bring in more people. A lot more.

Perhaps we should even take the time to re-organize ourselves and rethink our strategy."

"That's a sensible recommendation, Mr. Carson," said the Briton. "Unfortunately, time is something we can no longer afford. We'll have to make do with the resources currently at our disposal."

Carson looked worried. "In that case, sir, after what happened today, I can't say I'm very optimistic about our chances of success."

"Believe it or not, Mr. Carson, you were simply very unlucky. Soran's case is unique. We didn't expect him to be involved, at this point." Leicester paused and muttered to himself, "I'm actually quite surprised Arianne was able to enlist his help." He then turned back to Carson and said, "Still, you were warned not to engage the fugitives in an enclosed space. It puts you and your men at too much of a disadvantage. Why did you ignore this warning?"

"It was just one guy," said Carson. "Quite frankly, if I hadn't seen it for myself, I don't know if I would have believed it."

"Well, now you know why Soran wasn't included in your list of targets. In any case, in the future, I suggest you adhere to our recommendations when dealing with our young friends. It's best to try to apprehend them individually, whenever possible. And to confront them in an open area, where your men can neutralize them from a safe distance. Finally, and this goes without saying but, whatever you do, never confront them one-on-one. I'm afraid even someone as capable as you would not survive such an encounter."

"It'll be hard enough just to find them," said Carson. "How are we supposed to get them all gift-wrapped like that?"

"That, Mr. Carson, is precisely why we need the analyst. With her predictive abilities, she could anticipate their actions, and allow us to be better prepared."

Carson looked skeptical. "Sir, even if we somehow got the girl back, I doubt she'd want to help us. I only saw her from a distance, but I didn't get the impression she was being held against her will. On the contrary, she seemed to get along fine with the rest of them."

"I know," said Leicester. "But with the right incentive, I'm confident she could be persuaded to cooperate with us once again. She cares about her family above all else. Given the choice, she would rather see them in our care, than killed or captured by a less scrupulous organization."

Carson's gaze grew sharper. "You're referring to WIAS?"

A faint smile escaped Leicester. "Quick to catch on as always, I see. Good. Next time, make sure you follow protocol when dealing with the fugitives. Besides, Mr. Jenkins is in charge of this operation. Under normal circumstances, he would have been the one to lead the assault. Which, as you know, would have significantly improved your chances of success."

"I can't argue with that," said Carson. "Where is Patrick, anyway? I haven't been able to reach him for some time."

"There was an incident in London. It seems that while everyone else was busy here in Paris, someone organized a little excursion to one of my offices. The guards reported seeing two men and a woman whose descriptions match Damien, Arianne, and Mr. Kincade. I asked Mr. Jenkins to look into the matter."

"Really? What were they doing there?"

"The same thing we're all doing, Mr. Carson. Searching for Adam's data card. They broke into a storage room where we've been keeping some of the subject's belongings. My people inventoried the items and informed me that a necklace is missing. It's safe to assume this necklace is an important piece in the search for the hidden card. To think it's been right under our noses from the beginning. It's quite embarrassing, really."

"Does that mean those three are working together?"

Leicester shook his head. "No. It's actually the opposite. The report states that the intruders fought against one another. In fact, that's how the guards became aware of their presence. This confirms what we've known since Lucielle's abduction. The subjects have split up into two factions. One led by Damien, and the other by Arianne."

"Did the report mention anything else?" Carson asked.

"Indeed. It would appear Arianne and Mr. Kincade left before Damien did. This would suggest that they acquired the necklace and then managed to get away from him. At this point, that's the only silver lining."

"I don't understand," said Carson. "Why would it matter which one of them got the necklace? Isn't the outcome the same for us, either way?"

Leicester's expression turned grave. "Mr. Carson, let there be absolutely no doubt in your mind that Damien poses the greatest threat to our interests. That's why you were given a special directive in regards to him. The order stands: Neutralize on sight, by any means necessary."

"Understood, sir."

"The same applies to Johann," said Leicester. "The military has always shown a special interest in him, but they don't realize they'll never be able to control him. He's too far gone."

At that moment, there was a knock on the door.

One of the agents posted outside walked into the room. "Sorry to disturb you, sir. We've just been notified that the surgery was almost over. The doctor should be available within the next few minutes."

"Good," said Leicester. "Send someone to fetch him as soon as he leaves the operating room."

"Yes, sir."

Carson waited for the agent to leave and then turned to his employer. "What was that about, sir?"

Leicester walked over to the desk and absent-mindedly began to flip through some documents. "There's a reason I requested you and your men be brought to this hospital, Mr. Carson. It's come to my attention that one of the patients here is someone who could prove useful to us."

"A patient?"

"Yes. He was admitted under an alias, but it wasn't hard to discover who he was."

"Who is he?" Carson asked. "And how can he help us?"

"Patience, Mr. Carson. I intended to brief both you and Mr. Jenkins on this new development." Leicester checked his watch. "In truth, I expected Mr. Jenkins to have returned from London by now. I wonder what's keeping him," he added with a pensive frown.

"Sir, about Patrick …"

Leicester raised an eyebrow at his associate. "Yes?"

"I mean … it could be nothing …"

Whatever Carson had in mind, he was obviously reluctant to talk about it. Which only piqued Leicester's curiosity even more. "Well, what is it?" the Briton asked.

"Something strange happened at that hotel," Carson finally declared.

Leicester was intrigued. "Strange how? Please, elaborate."

Chapter 15 – You Can't Be Serious

When Professor Fournier walked by the living room as he headed to the kitchen, he saw Lucielle and Marie seated together on the large sofa. The young girl was leaning back comfortably and aiming the remote control at the television as she flipped through the channels. She didn't seem to notice that the detective was staring at her with a frozen look of disbelief on her face.

"How are you two getting along?" Fournier asked, wondering what accounted for Marie's strange expression.

"We're fine," Lucielle replied, her eyes fixed on the screen. "Oh, and I told Marie about us," she added nonchalantly.

Fournier studied the detective briefly and said, "I see …"

Marie stood up and approached him. "You see?" she whispered, making sure the young girl couldn't hear her. "Do you have any idea what she said?"

"Judging from the look on your face, I'm pretty sure she told you the truth," the old man calmly replied.

When she heard the professor's remark, Lucielle turned her head. She rose from the sofa and walked over to the pair. "You thought I was lying?" she asked, peering up at the detective.

"Of course not, sweetie," Marie replied in a gentle voice. "I'm sure you believe everything you told me. It's just … even for grown-ups, things can sometimes appear so complicated that it becomes easy to get confused. It's true there's a lot I still don't understand, but … genetically enhanced people? … and clones? I'm sure there's a more reasonable explanation."

Marie eyed the professor to observe his reaction. Now that he knew what he had so carelessly endorsed, she expected him to brush off Lucielle's outrageous claims as nothing more than the wild musings of a child with an overactive imagination. The detective was convinced this was the young girl's way of coping with a difficult and stressful situation.

But when the professor responded with an approving nod, Marie's jaw literally dropped to the floor. Yet again, she found herself questioning the old man's sanity.

"You can't be serious!" she exclaimed. "Human clones?"

"Yes," Fournier vigorously nodded.

Very slowly, Marie's eyes rolled down towards Lucielle. "You're a ..."

"I am," Lucielle replied. "And so are my brothers and sisters."

The detective needed a moment. She sat on the sofa's armrest because she no longer trusted her legs to hold her up.

"I realize how awkward this must seem, at first," said Fournier. "But don't worry, in time, you'll get used to the idea."

Marie tittered at his remark. "Get used to it? I don't know, it sounds a lot like science fiction to me."

"Sure, I can understand that," he said. "But when you think about it, science fiction is nothing more than science that hasn't been discovered yet."

The detective seemed to concede that point, but there was still a lingering glimmer of doubt in her eyes. "So, you and Professor Karpov … you … what? cloned them?"

"No, that was Lucielle's father," Fournier replied.

Suddenly, Marie looked even more confused. "Father? But, you just said …"

"Lucielle and her siblings were created by a man named Adam Cross," the professor explained. "And he cloned them using his own DNA. Which, for all intents and purposes, makes them his children. Damien and Lucielle are exact replicas of Adam. That's why they've inherited his last name: Cross. The others were the result of a more elaborate cloning method, but most of their DNA also comes from Adam."

During her time as a detective, Marie had occasionally come across crime scenes which, on initial inspection, appeared to defy all logic and reason. But experience had taught her that, in the end, there was always a rational explanation waiting to be dug up from under every heap of the bizarre and the unexplained. And despite everything she had witnessed in the past couple of days, deep down, she still believed this time would be no different. She thought once the curtains were lifted, they would reveal a neat little trick to explain away all the illusions.

She was wrong.

Fournier gave the detective a long, probing look.

She was still a little dazed from the incredible revelation, but all things considered, she was dealing with it well enough. He believed the events from earlier in the day had made it easier for her to accept this extraordinary new reality.

Lucielle also had the same impression. She could see the barriers gradually crumble behind the detective's eyes as more pieces of the puzzle came together in her mind.

All of a sudden, Marie whipped her head around towards the professor. "Wait a minute! Is any of this even legal?"

Fournier's eyes shifted away. "Well … of course, from a legal perspective, we may have … cut a few corners here and there," he said, struggling to answer her question.

The detective squinted suspiciously. "Hmm, that doesn't sound very convincing," she said.

"You make a valid point," Lucielle interjected. "But I'm afraid in this case, it wouldn't have made any difference."

Marie tilted her head at the young girl.

"As I mentioned earlier," Lucielle continued. "The research in question was instigated by informal branches of the governments of three West European countries, in partnership with the US Military. From their perspective, this wasn't just another interesting venture, but rather a necessary one. Therefore, and taking into consideration the nature of the parties involved, it would be naïve to expect them to have desisted from this research purely out of ethical, or even legal, concerns."

For the third or fourth time that day, Marie stared at the strange young girl with a mix of surprise and confusion. Part of her stupefaction stemmed from having been called *naïve* by an eleven-year-old child. But mostly, she couldn't believe how grave and mature that child had sounded. Even the tone of Lucielle's voice had changed. In that instant, Marie could not find a trace of the innocent-looking girl who had been humming with insouciance as she brushed her doll's hair.

Mistakenly believing that Marie's reaction was a result of her taking offense at Lucielle's directness, Professor Fournier thought it best to take over.

"You must keep in mind," he said, "that once a discovery has been made, it cannot be *undiscovered*. The genie can't be put back into the bottle, so to speak. Those who would abandon all research in a particular field, be it for legal or moral reasons, have but two options. One: trust that others will not continue that research in secret. Or two: run the risk of finding themselves at a disadvantage, should some other party achieve a major breakthrough. Having spent most of my life working for the kinds of people we're talking about here, I can guarantee that you won't find a more paranoid bunch anywhere. *Trust,* simply isn't part of their world view."

Suddenly, the doorbell rang.

Chapter 16 – Tension

"Ah! They're here," said Fournier as he got up and went to answer the door.

Having heard the doorbell as well, Doc showed up in the entrance hall, gun in hand, and joined the professor.

"It's all right," the old man told him. "It's just Arianne and your friend. She called me to let me know they were near-by. I was waiting for them."

Lucielle and Marie also moved closer as Fournier opened the door.

As soon as Arianne walked in, her sister ran into her arms and asked, "Are you all right?"

"I'm fine, Luce," Arianne replied.

"I was so worried when they told me Damien was there," the young girl said.

"That certainly made the trip more interesting," Kincade remarked. "But then again, you guys had plenty of excitement too."

"We sure did," said Doc.

"I'm sorry," Marie said in a timid voice. "Those men probably followed me to the professor's home."

"You must be that German detective Doc told me about," said Kincade. "Don't worry about it. For all we know, they found that place on their own. Hi, my name's Nate," he said, holding out his hand.

"Hi, I'm Marie. Nice to meet you," she replied as they exchanged a cordial handshake.

Arianne approached the detective but remained beyond arm's reach. "Hello," she said.

At first, Marie couldn't help but stare in silence—she was still a little numb from learning the truth about Lucielle and her siblings. But she eventually returned the greeting, "Hello."

"You told my friends that you knew Professor Karpov?" Arianne asked.

"Yes, we met a couple of years ago. But we spent a lot of time together after that. He was a truly dear friend."

"May I ask why you've come to Paris?"

Arianne's tone was neutral, but her eyes projected a blend of kindness and sadness that reminded Marie of Professor Karpov. Normally, that familiar feeling would have put the detective more at ease. But oddly, what she felt was the complete opposite. Though she did not quite know why, Arianne's gaze elicited a growing sense of unease within her.

"I'm here because Professor Karpov was my friend," said Marie. "I want to get justice for his murder."

"Don't you mean revenge?" Arianne corrected.

"No ... maybe ... I don't know. All I know is that I can't just sit around in Berlin and pretend that nothing happened."

Arianne paused and sighed. "By now, you must be aware of the rare dangers you'll have to face if you choose to stay with us."

"I guess," said the detective. "But it's too late for me to turn back. Too many people know about me. I doubt I'll be safe even if I return to Berlin now. I have no choice but to see this through."

Arianne's scrutinizing gaze did not relent.

Marie felt as though this woman, whom she had never met before, could somehow peer behind her pupils and shine a light inside the deepest recesses of her mind. It was an odd sensation. One she imagined was similar to being naked in front of a stranger.

This feeling of discomfort caused the detective to avert her eyes, almost as a protective reflex. That's when she noticed Lucielle and Professor Fournier staring at her with a strange anticipation. It was like they were waiting for something to happen.

Kincade and Doc remained silent as well. They understood the reason for the other's sudden stillness. They remembered that Arianne's heightened empathic sense allowed her to detect all forms of deception. This talent had already been demonstrated to them when they had questioned Leicester's assistant, Mark Stanwell.

And now, it was Marie's turn.

After all, what did they really know about this detective from Berlin? She had shown up out of nowhere to Professor Fournier's home, with Carson's squad right on her heels. What if it had all been part of some elaborate plot? She could have been planted in their midst as a spy. A failsafe, in case Carson's assault failed. Leicester could have briefed her on what to say.

In view of their recent setbacks, neither Kincade's team nor the fugitives could afford another misstep. Fortunately for them, Arianne would be able to tell whether or not the detective was telling the truth.

Of course, Leicester would have been aware of that fact. But it wasn't beyond the realm of possibilities that he would have taken the chance anyway.

With all eyes intently fixed on her, Marie's unease quickly turned into apprehension. She could tell something was going on, but what exactly? Her right hand instinctively inched closer to the gun holstered on her waist as she cast a nervous glance around her.

But when the detective's gaze landed back on the woman in front of her, she noticed something had changed. The piercing intensity had faded from Arianne's eyes.

"I apologize if I've made you nervous," Arianne said with a smile. "It's a pleasure to meet you." She extended her hand to the blond woman.

Marie tentatively shook it and said, "Pleasure to meet you, too."

Just like that, the tension in the air was gone. The detective was bewildered to see that everyone had abruptly stopped paying attention to her. Doc and Kincade exchanged some words as they moved away, while Lucielle and the professor bombarded Arianne with questions. *What just happened?* Marie wondered.

"I'll tell you everything," Arianne said as she pulled away from Lucielle and Fournier. "But first, I'd like to go check on Ash and Soran."

"I'll go with you," said the young girl as she followed her sister into the right-hand side corridor.

"Would anyone like something to eat, or drink?" Fournier asked out of the blue.

The mercenaries shook their heads. But Marie took him up on his offer. With everything that had been going on, she hadn't had a chance to eat anything since early the morning.

"I wouldn't mind a bite," she said.

"In that case, follow me, young lady," Fournier said as he led her into the kitchen. "There isn't much, but I'm sure we can at least fix you a sandwich."

Left alone, the two mercenaries sat down in the living room.

"It took you a while to get back from London," Doc remarked.

"Couldn't be helped," said Kincade. "We needed to be extra careful. Leicester's men were searching for us all over the city."

"Oh, I see."

"Is Da Costa going to be OK?" Kincade asked, sounding worried.

"I think so," Doc replied. "Thankfully, we got him to a hospital fairly quickly."

Kincade breathed a sigh of relief. "I'm glad to hear it. Still, we'll have to get him out of there, soon. The longer he stays in that place, the greater the risk Leicester will find out about him."

"I know," said Doc. "But before we can do that, we'll need to know how his surgery went, and if it's safe to move him."

"How? We can't exactly show up and ask for an update."

"Soran might be able to hack into their network," Doc suggested. "He specializes in that kind of stuff, doesn't he?" He paused and then added, "Well, that's assuming he doesn't try to kill us again."

"Soran, eh?" Kincade chuckled. "Was it really that bad?"

"Worse," Doc said. "Believe me, this is no laughing matter. If it hadn't been for Lucielle, some of us wouldn't have made it. Hell, maybe none of us would have."

Kincade shook his head in disbelief. "I have to admit," he said. "I'm having a hard time wrapping my head around this one. I mean, I was almost worried for the guy. He didn't look like he could handle himself in a tough situation."

"I know what you mean. It was a shock for me, too. He seemed like the least threatening of them all, aside from the kid, of course."

"You buy that multiple personality crap?"

"Absolutely!" Doc replied without hesitation. "You didn't see him, back there. That was definitely someone else."

Kincade paused to think. "This complicates things."

"You're telling me?" said Doc.

Kincade exhaled heavily and said, "I'm gonna go see what Rock and Sonar are up to. Later on, we should have a meeting to figure out our next move."

"All right," said Doc. "But at some point, you and I need to have a little talk." His expression had turned grave.

"Sounds serious," said Kincade. "Can it wait a bit?"

"Sure. A bit."

Carson silently stood in the middle of the room as he carefully studied every detail of Andrew Leicester's face. Over the years, he'd had several opportunities to observe his employer during times of crises. A man in Leicester's position shouldered a great number of responsibilities. The decisions he made often had long-lasting and far-reaching consequences. And as part of his duties—both formal and informal—the British diplomat was often asked to resolve complex issues within unreasonable time frames.

And yet, however dire the circumstances, or seemingly impossible the tasks, one thing had always remained constant: Leicester's immutable facade. He always exuded an unassailable self-confidence. A sense of being in control, epitomized by his smile. That quasi-permanent, knowing smile, which revealed nothing, but gave the impression he knew exactly what the other parties were thinking, and what was going to happen next. *I wouldn't want to play poker with him*, Carson had thought many times.

But as he gazed at his employer now, Carson could not recall a time when he had seen such a concerned look on the Briton's face.

Leicester was leaning back against the desk and drumming his fingers on the edge as he stared pensively into space.

All of a sudden, he stopped and shifted his gaze back to Carson. "Have you reported this to anyone?" he asked.

"No," Carson replied. "I had intended to ask Patrick about it, first."

"Don't," Leicester told him. "In fact, don't mention it to anyone else. It's imperative this stays between us."

"Understood, sir."

At that moment, there was another knock on the door.

The same agent as earlier came in and stood at the entrance. "The doctor has arrived, sir."

Leicester straightened up and nodded.

The agent moved aside to make way for a man in blue scrubs.

The doctor walked in and glanced back as the agent closed the door behind him. Then, he turned to face the two men waiting inside the office and asked, "Who are you?"

"My name's Andrew Leicester," the Brit replied. "And this is my associate, Mr. Randall Carson." His smile had returned, clearing away all traces of worry.

The doctor eyed them a moment longer. Their names, like their faces, meant absolutely nothing to him. "Why was I brought here?" he asked, in a wary tone.

"My good doctor," said Leicester. "I do apologize for asking you here in such an indelicate manner."

"Asking? You're joking, right?" the doctor said. "Those men outside practically dragged me out of surgery and escorted me here like I was some sort of criminal."

"Again," said Leicester. "You have my sincere apologies. But we need your help with an urgent matter."

The doctor crossed his arms over his chest. "There's no need to be so condescending," he said. "I received a call from the head of the board of directors when I was in the O.R. He told me, and I quote: 'to provide any and all assistance required of his guest'."

"Good," said Leicester. "I'm sure we'll get along splendidly." He then turned to his associate. "Mr. Carson, meet Doctor Philippe Laplace."

Chapter 17 – Beneath the Surface

Professor Fournier and Detective Heirtmeyer returned to the living room and found all four mercenaries waiting for them. Rock was leaning against the doorframe between the living room and the dining room, with Sonar standing next to him. Doc had taken a seat at the far end of the three-seater sofa, and Kincade had straddled a chair facing the entrance hall. He had spun it around and had placed his elbows atop the backrest.

Upon seeing them, the professor stopped and lowered his glass, just as he was about to take a sip of apple cider.

Marie, who was a couple of steps behind him and holding a glass of the same drink, halted as well.

"We have a few questions to ask you," Kincade declared.

"Yes," said Fournier. "I imagine you do."

"And *we* have some questions of our own," said Arianne as she walked into the living room, followed by Lucielle and Soran, whom they had let out of his restraints.

Marie gasped when she saw the young man. Her entire body tensed up and the glass slipped from her fingers.

By the time the glass hit the floor and shattered into a dozen pieces, three of the four mercenaries had drawn their weapons and were aiming them at Soran.

Arianne quickly moved in front of her brother and raised both hands in an appeasing gesture. "Please! I understand," she said. "But it's safe now. I assure you."

Kincade promptly stood up, surprised by his team's reaction. "Whoa! Calm down, guys. What are you all doing?"

"No offense, Nate," his redheaded comrade told him. "But you weren't there. That guy's a walking natural disaster."

"That's right!" Rock emphatically agreed. "He's all kinds of crazy. And I don't mean '*therapist crazy*', either. We're talking seriously messed up, here."

"It's not a good idea to scare him like that," Lucielle chimed.

But no one was paying much attention to her.

Soran slowly pushed Arianne aside and gazed at the group. "Look, I'm sorry about what happened back there," he told them.

"I'm sorry too," said the redhead. "But '*sorry*' just ain't gonna cut it."

"He did save us from those men who attacked us," Fournier pointed out.

"You mean those poor bastards he butchered?" Rock countered. "Yeah, that's very reassuring."

Doc Chen, who had been just as quick as the other two to draw his firearm, observed Soran at length. Then, without a word, he calmly holstered his weapon.

"What are you doing, Doc?" Rock asked in a surprised tone of voice.

"I think we can relax, for now," he replied.

"Speak for yourself," the giant threw back.

"That's enough," Kincade told his two comrades. "Put your guns away."

Rock and Sonar glanced at each other with their firearms still raised.

"Now!" Kincade barked.

They hesitated for a second longer, and then reluctantly complied.

Rock then walked over to Soran. "Just so we're clear," he said as he poked the young man on the chest. "If you so much as look at me funny … I'm gonna shoot you."

Soran frowned and poked him back. "Hey! I'm trying to apologize here," he said. "Besides, from what I hear, you *did* shoot me."

"You were being a jerk," said the giant.

"That wasn't me. That was Myrvan."

"Oh, yeah? Then I didn't shoot you, did I? I shot Myrvan."

Soran opened his mouth, intending to come up with a sharp riposte. But nothing came to mind. What could one find to say to that?

Kincade moved between them and gently pushed his comrade away.

"All right, you've made your point," he told the giant. "Now get back to where you were."

Arianne placed her hand on her brother's shoulder and said in a soft voice, "You too, Soran. Go check on Ash, OK?"

"But I was only trying to apologize," he meekly protested.

"I know," she said. "Now, listen to your older sister. Go on."

"Fine," he replied.

As he watched Soran turn around and drag his feet towards the hallway, Doc recalled the events from earlier that afternoon. It was strange to think that the vicious killer who had so mercilessly slaughtered Carson's squad, and this young man who had essentially just been sent back to his room, were, in fact, the same person.

"Shouldn't someone keep an eye on him?" the redhead suggested.

"Don't worry," said Fournier. "He'll be fine."

"Uh … it's not exactly him we're worried about," Rock remarked.

"It's extremely rare for Myrvan to come out," said Arianne. "You're not likely to see it again anytime soon."

"That's right," Lucielle agreed. "Just, try not to scare him, OK?"

"What does that even mean?" the giant said in an annoyed voice.

During the entire scene, Marie had remained silent. Even though the professor had tried to make her feel like a member of the group, in reality, she was still an outsider. Those people were all strangers to her. With the exception of Professor Fournier, she didn't even know any of them existed twenty-four hours ago.

She crouched down, and carefully started picking up the pieces of glass scattered around her.

"Let me help you with that," said Arianne as she knelt down next to the detective and began collecting shards of glass. She then looked up at her sister and said, "Luce, go to the kitchen and look for something we can use to clean this up, will you?"

The young girl ran off, and returned seconds later, holding a stack of tissue paper and a biodegradable plastic bag.

She handed the items to her sister.

"Thank you," said the young woman.

"Can I help, too?" Lucielle asked.

"No," Arianne replied. "You might cut yourself. Go sit with Nate."

"Come take a seat next to me, Luce," Kincade called to her.

Lucielle ran around the two-seater sofa—to get to the side closest to Kincade—and sank into it.

Nate. Luce. Doc felt his brow twitch as he noted the growing familiarity between Kincade and Arianne. But he refrained from commenting on it.

Professor Fournier turned to the mercenary leader. "What is it you wanted to ask me, young man?"

Before Kincade could respond, Sonar held up his index finger and turned to Arianne with a puzzled frown. "Hold on, back up," he said. "Why did you call yourself Soran's *older sister*?"

She gave the redhead a blank stare. As if his question didn't make sense.

Fournier also gazed at the mercenary with a similar expression. "Uh … because she's older than him," the professor finally replied.

"Older?" Kincade echoed, picking-up on his comrade's remark. "I thought you were all the same age. Except for the kid, of course."

Arianne turned to him, looking surprised. "Why would you think that?" she asked.

"Well, you're clones, aren't you?" Rock blurted out.

Lucielle frowned at him. "Yeah, and?"

The mood inside the living room immediately turned heavier as everyone feared they would have to endure yet another tiresome squabble between the giant and the young girl.

Eager to avoid this outcome, Professor Fournier hastened his explanation. "Almost all the clones were created individually," he said. "And at about a one-year interval. Damien was the first. It makes sense, since he's an exact replica of Adam, and the result of a cell-cloning procedure. The transgenic method used for the others probably took more time to perfect. A year after Damien, was Darius. And about a year after him, Arianne. But Ashrem followed only two months after her."

"Oh, why is that?" Kincade asked.

"For some reason, Adam used almost the same genetic material for the both of them. Which may explain the strange connection they've always shared," Fournier commented. "And after another year, there was the twins."

"Twins?" Doc said.

"Johann and Kadyna. They're twins."

"Was that by design?" Doc asked.

"I'm not sure," said the old man. "I think so. Next, came Mitsuki. And finally, Soran."

"What about Lucielle?" Marie asked. "Why is she so much younger?"

"Lucielle is different from her brothers and sisters," the professor replied. "Let's just leave it at that, for now."

"Why wait a year each time?" Kincade wondered aloud.

"I asked Adam that same question, once," said Fournier. "He explained to me that due to the intricate nature of the cloning process, the potential for complications was very high, particularly during the first year. He wanted to make sure there were no major issues during that sensitive period before trying again."

Rock chuckled. "Well, that was a total bust."

"Why do you say that?" Lucielle asked in a belligerent voice.

"Why do you think?" the giant retorted. "Each one of you turned out to be a bigger nut job than the previous ones. Clearly, something went wrong."

"Come on, man," said Sonar. "That's a little harsh, isn't it?"

"Harsh? Oh, I don't know," said the giant. "Personally, I think when her brother tried to kill us all, back there … now *that* was harsh."

"Ahem! In any case," Fournier continued. "Despite Adam's best efforts, he fully expected his children would have to face certain personal challenges. It was unavoidable. As I previously explained to you, he knew his desire to pass on, not only his physical capabilities, but his mental aptitudes as well, would result in his children having to deal with some kind of psychological disorder. Just as he had."

"And yet, he did it anyway?" said Doc.

"Maybe he chose to believe that, like him, they'd be able to overcome those hurdles in time."

"And, will they?" Doc asked.

The old man shook his head. "I don't know. Adam started the Eritis project because he wanted to create others like himself. And for all intents and purposes, he succeeded. However, in spite of everything they can do, his children are not as gifted as he was. Not even Damien."

"How can that be?" said Kincade. "I thought Adam and Damien were identical."

"They are," said the professor. "And yet, somehow … they're not. Remember, no one ever understood why or how Adam turned out the way he did. Sure, Professor Engel's goal was to create more advanced human beings. Which he ultimately did. But as I told you before, from a purely scientific point of view, his experiment failed. Only four out of several hundred test subjects made it past the first phase. And even Professor Engel himself could not explain why those four had survived. On top of that, one of them possessed an intellect far beyond anything the professor had ever thought possible. That in itself was also a great mystery. In truth, I don't expect we'll ever see someone else like Adam."

Fournier marked a brief pause and then muttered, "Well ... probably not ... that is."

"What is it now?" Rock asked in an irritated voice. "Just spit it out, Pops."

Feeling the need to shield the professor from reproach, Arianne intervened. "It's a little complicated," she said. "Adam believed that one of us had the potential to surpass him. It's just ... no one knows for sure."

"Yes, the potential is definitely there," Fournier enthusiastically nodded. "Unfortunately, we never got the chance to properly evaluate him."

"Him? Are you talking about Damien?" Kincade asked.

Arianne and Fournier exchanged a quick glance.

The young woman stood back up, along with the detective—they had finished cleaning the floor and had gathered all glass fragments into the plastic bag. She then looked at Kincade and shook her head.

At that point, Arianne no longer needed to spell it out for the others. Hers and the professor's silence had spoken volumes. It didn't take long for the mercenaries to guess the answer.

"Please tell me you're not talking about Soran," Rock said with a resigned expression.

But then, to his entire team's surprise, Lucielle turned to him and declared, "They're not."

Puzzled gazes immediately converged on the young analyst.

She glanced around, genuinely surprised to see them look so confused. "Really. They're not," she repeated. "They're talking about Myrvan."

Marie promptly covered her mouth to smother the laugh that was about to escape her. Lucielle's declaration had been so unexpected, and her expression so innocent, so sincere, that the detective had found it adorably amusing.

But then again, Marie had only been with the group for a few hours. And in spite of everything she had been told, when the detective looked at Lucielle, all she saw was an adolescent girl with strange silver-grey hair.

Unlike Marie, however, the mercenaries had had more time to get acquainted with Lucielle's less endearing personality traits.

As he gazed at the youngster, Kincade exhaled tiredly and shook his head. A reaction that summed up the general mood among his team, with one notable, yet unsurprising, exception.

"You … I swear …" Rock said as he gritted his teeth. It was like the words themselves had become too painful to articulate.

The giant looked so scary that Lucielle sprang from the sofa, ran over to Arianne, and hid behind her.

"Is this your idea of a joke?" Rock finally yelled at her.

"It's not a joke," Lucielle replied as she stuck out her head while clinging to her sister's waist.

"Soran, Marvin … who cares?" Rock bellowed. "It's the same damn thing!"

"No, it's not," the girl shouted back. "And his name is Myrvan, not Marvin."

"All right, that's it! I'm gonna squeeze your scrawny little neck," the giant threatened as he marched towards her.

"Come on, big guy," Doc said. "You know we don't have time for this."

The huge mercenary halted his advance and pointed a menacing finger at Lucielle before returning to his spot in the doorway.

"And you, stop antagonizing him," Arianne told her sister. "Come on, let's go sit down." She turned to Marie and added, "You should have a seat, as well."

Professor Fournier motioned the detective to come sit near him on the large sofa. "Please."

Marie took a seat between the old man and Doc Chen. While Lucielle returned to the two-seater, along with Arianne.

"Don't be afraid, kid," said Kincade. "Rock may look scary, but he only hurts bad people."

The giant grunted and looked away.

"It's not his fault, you know," said Lucielle.

"Who? Rock?" Kincade asked.

"No, my brother. It's not his fault that he's like this."

"Yeah, yeah," Rock said, sounding unsympathetic. "You were all imprisoned for a really long time and they did all kinds of weird experiments on you. We got it. But I don't see the rest of you try to murder everyone because of that."

"No, you don't understand," said Lucielle. "It was different for him."

Kincade turned to Arianne, squinting as he searched his memory. "I remember you saying something similar the night we met with Soran, in that music bar. What do you guys mean? Different how?"

"Perhaps, I should be the one to clarify," Fournier interjected.

Rock rolled his eyes. "Argh, here we go. You really like giving long lectures, don't you?"

It wasn't the first time that Rock had called attention to the professor's propensity to indulge in profuse explanations. It made Fournier a bit defensive. And he felt the need to justify himself. "It's just that, as one of the lead scientists at the Arc, I had access to information which Arianne and her siblings weren't privy to. Not to mention they were only children when some of those events took place."

"Don't mind him, professor," Sonar said, sensing the old man's embarrassment.

"Yeah, pops! Don't mind me," said Rock. "Go on. Clarify away."

The professor straightened up in his seat and paused to make sure he had everyone's attention.

"Look how happy he is," Rock whispered to his redheaded comrade.

"Shut up," Sonar whispered back.

"You see," Fournier began. "As a child, Myrvan wasn't—"

"Don't you mean Soran?" Kincade interrupted.

"I beg your pardon?" said the old man.

"You said, 'as a child'. You meant Soran, right?"

Fournier stared at him at length before turning to Arianne and Lucielle.

The same look of realization washed over the trio's faces.

"That's right," Arianne muttered. "We never said."

Doc frowned with apprehension. "Never said what?"

"Soran," she said. "His persona only appeared about eight years ago. The one we grew up with ... it was Myrvan."

Arianne paused when she saw the look on Kincade's face.

He was shocked. But also irritated that he hadn't been told something so significant.

She understood his reaction, and even felt bad about it. She knew she ought to have mentioned it sooner. But it had been an honest mistake, not a deception. To Arianne and her family—which included Professor Fournier—Soran was also one of Adam's children. The same as the others. Which was why it hadn't occurred to any of them to bring up his past.

Arianne accepted that Kincade would be upset. But after she cast an eye over the rest of the group, she realized his was not the reaction she needed to worry about the most.

Kincade's comrades, as well as Marie, had all been equally stunned by what they had just heard. But having witnessed first-hand the carnage and mayhem caused by Myrvan in just a few short minutes, their astonishment soon gave way to far less benign sentiments.

When Arianne scrutinized the three mercenaries and the detective, she could almost hear the cogs turning inside their heads as the full implications of her statement began to dawn on them.

She sensed their anxiety and their misgivings. But most of all, she sensed their fear.

A deadly threat that had been described to them as distant and unlikely, suddenly seemed much closer and much more pressing. None of them had been particularly thrilled at the idea of staying in the same apartment as someone they considered to be a ticking time bomb. And that was when they thought the monster was hibernating in the depths of Soran's consciousness. But as it turned out, he was merely dozing off just beneath the surface.

Aware of the tension rising inside the room, Lucielle tried to reassure everyone once again. "It's OK," she said. "You don't need to worry. We're all safe, now."

"How is any of this OK?" Rock said. "You've just told us that 'rampaging killer psycho' is pretty much his default mode."

Sonar stepped forward and declared, "I hate to say it, but I agree with the big guy. This isn't funny."

"Aren't you guys overreacting a little?" Kincade asked.

"You didn't see the bodies in that living room," said Doc. "Or what happened after that. It seems to me this situation is far more serious than our *friends* would have us believe." He turned to the professor and added, "If Myrvan's the main personality, then I don't see how any of you can guarantee he won't show up again to finish what he started."

"We know Myrvan won't re-emerge," said Fournier. "Because he doesn't want to."

"Do you people always have to be so damned cryptic?" Rock said in an exasperated tone of voice.

"If you would bear with me a little," Fournier said. "The only way to make you understand is to start from the beginning." He shot a quick glance at Rock and added, "I'll try not to be too long."

Chapter 18 – Secret

The professor explained that, as a child, Myrvan had always been aloof and introverted. Initially, everyone had thought that he had been afflicted with the same condition as Mitsuki: the inability to process emotions. But in time, it became clear the boy's anti-social tendencies were a personality trait rather than a psychological impairment. It wasn't that he didn't know how to communicate his feelings to others, it was just that he didn't want to. At least, not to everyone. He only truly opened up when he was alone with his siblings or their father, and on occasion, with Professors Karpov and Fournier.

A few military-appointed psychiatrists, and other so-called children specialists, had been brought in to analyze him. But, predictably enough, every single one of them had failed at their assignment.

Eventually, the specialists stopped coming. And Myrvan was simply categorized as one of the least responsive subjects. And that was that. After all, there were other, less complicated, subjects to study.

And the boy still participated in every activity required of him. So what, if he was shy?

There was also another reason Myrvan had been able to get away with ignoring almost everyone around him. Adam.

In the project's early years, when their father was still with them, the children's everyday life was very different from what it would later become. Their situation back in those days could more accurately be described as a form of house arrest rather than an imprisonment. They were free to roam around the living quarters, labs, training rooms, kitchens, and other areas of the main building's sub-levels.

Obviously, they couldn't leave, or have any contact with the outside world. But Adam insisted his children be allowed to move around freely, and even be granted permission to play outside, on occasion. Of course, that latter request was met with some resistance from the military brass. Words like 'regulations' and 'protocol violations' constantly resurfaced in every discussion. But their father remained adamant. *Even convicted felons get to go outside from time to time,* he argued, a*nd those kids haven't done anything to anyone.*

Professors Fournier and Karpov sided with him. They pointed out that his proposal was necessary for the proper development of the subjects, which, in turn, would have a direct impact on their value to the project.

In the end, it was agreed that each day, under heavy surveillance, the children would get two hours outside, within the compound's limits. It wasn't ideal, but Adam knew it was the best he could hope for.

He also insisted that he be in charge of the children's education. Every subject and every lesson had to be pre-approved by a specially-assigned team, but Adam would be the one to teach them.

This had been an easy concession to obtain in view of the children's extraordinary learning capabilities. They were able to comprehend and extrapolate so much, based on so little information that, in truth, any other teacher would have quickly found themselves overwhelmed by such students. Though, at times, when he was too busy fulfilling his own duties, Adam would rely on his friends, Jerome Fournier and Aleksandr Karpov, to fill in for him. He trusted them. And they were the only other people for whom the children seemed to have any regard.

Just like their father, the children had a busy routine, and underwent weekly medical and psychological examinations. Their mental and physical aptitudes were tested on a regular basis via an endless series of puzzles, drills, exercises, and simulations. And from the age of five, they had been put through a rigorous combat training program, which included hand-to-hand fighting, weapons handling, and other specialist skills.

But as the children grew older, their strength increased to dangerous levels. The hand-to-hand combat training, in particular, became an increasingly delicate affair. By the time Damien and Darius were twelve- and eleven-years-old respectively, the best option was to have them spar against each other. The same later applied to the other kids, once they reached a similar age.

From the beginning, the scientists' main focus had been on Damien. He was the eldest, and the only true replica of Adam. He was seen as the most important test subject, and as the best chance of success for the project. An assumption validated by his test scores. His comparative performance graphs were higher than those of his siblings, even after compensating for the age difference. And he alone had inherited Adam's predictive ability. There was no doubt each of the children possessed both intellect and strength rivaling that of their father. But Damien was the closest.

Or so everyone thought.

It was Professor Karpov who first brought the peculiar observation to his friend's—Professor Fournier's—attention. He had noticed that Myrvan's test results always fell around the group's average, regardless of the activity. This was strange because, as Karpov pointed out, each child had exhibited a higher proficiency than the average in at least one specific area. Basically, each one had at least one thing that they could do better than all the others.

Out of curiosity, Fournier decided to investigate the reason for those odd results.

His first indication that Karpov's instincts had been correct came during the following strength and endurance session.

The children were asked to push back against a metallic panel that was moving towards them and generating an increasing amount of pressure, the goal being to hold off the panel for as long as they could.

As was always the case during this type of exercise, Damien and Darius notably outlasted their younger siblings. But having kept a close eye on Myrvan, Fournier realized the boy had only pretended to reach his limit. In fact, it seemed so obvious to the professor, that he even wondered how he hadn't noticed it before, in all the previous sessions.

Suddenly, Fournier glanced around nervously. *If he could see it, wouldn't his colleagues see it, as well?* There would be serious consequences if it became known that one of the children had deliberately skewed his test results.

Thankfully, the other scientists remained none the wiser.

It surprised Fournier, at first. But then he thought, *why would they notice?*

Even though they had spent countless hours studying the children, none of the other scientists had any real interactions with them. And this was especially true of Mitsuki and Myrvan. It occurred to Fournier the only reason he had been able to see through the boy's pretense was that he actually knew him on a personal level. He knew his habits, facial expressions, and a host of other details that help us shape our understanding of other people.

Fournier wondered what accounted for the boy's deception. He told his friend, Alek, what he had observed, and they both agreed to keep it a secret.

But they had to let Adam know. Myrvan was his child. He would decide what to do about him.

After the death of Professor Engel, Adam made a deal with the project's overseers. In exchange for his many contributions, he would have total autonomy over his lab. Of course, scientists and security personnel would still have access to it, but not to his research. All important documents were kept inside a safe fitted with a biometric lock, and all computers files were protected by a software encryption which Adam himself had created.

Before it was agreed, that deal had been the subject of many acrimonious debates. A lot of people had questioned the wisdom in granting him that level of autonomy. But the top decision-makers were concerned with one thing above all else: results. And as long as Adam delivered on his commitments, they were willing to overlook his *eccentricities*. Besides, the project's scientists had themselves admitted, and on numerous occasions, that most of Adam's research was far beyond them. Why upset the balance of a beneficial arrangement just so some frustrated scientists could have a look at files which they couldn't really understand anyway?

The following day, when Fournier went to see Adam in his lab, he found him writing on a big whiteboard and thinking aloud. Fournier was about to call out to him when he noticed Myrvan standing at the other end of the whiteboard, with a marker in his hand.

The only presence Adam tolerated when he worked inside his lab was that of his children. Myrvan, in particular, seemed to spend a lot of time there, far more than his siblings. Like everyone else, Fournier had assumed that since Myrvan was his youngest—aside from Lucielle who was still a baby at the time—Adam indulged him more, and allowed the boy to disturb him more frequently, even while he worked.

Fournier had never really paid too much attention to Myrvan whenever he had found him inside his father's lab. But that time, the professor decided to wait and observe. Father and son were so focused on the arcane numbers and symbols on the board that neither of them noticed him standing at the entrance.

From what Fournier could tell, Adam was working on some theory related to gravity. But those calculations were so far over the professor's head that he couldn't even be sure.

One thing, however, did become clear to Fournier as he continued to observe the pair. The professor realized that Adam wasn't thinking aloud as he had previously believed. But that the silver-haired man was, in fact, talking to Myrvan. He was bouncing ideas back and forth with his son, as he would with an assistant.

Impossible, Fournier thought to himself.

"Oh, professor!" Adam exclaimed when he finally spotted him. "What are you doing standing over there?"

But Fournier didn't reply. Instead, he just kept staring at the boy with a strange expression.

"Is something wrong?" Adam asked.

Before Fournier could say anything, a young girl strode into the room, carrying a baby. She walked past the professor and went straight to Myrvan.

"There you are!" she said. "I knew it."

Adam smiled. "Have you come to get your brother, Arianne?"

"Yes," the young girl replied. "He's late for a simulation."

"I see. Well, go on, then," Adam said to his son.

Myrvan pouted. "Do I have to? Those are boring."

Arianne scowled at her brother. "Yes, you have to. We all do. We've already discussed this. Now stop being such a baby. Let's go!"

Adam's smile widened. "Speaking of babies," he said. "Do you want me to take Luce?"

"No, it's OK," said Arianne. "I can look after her. I'm free for the rest of the afternoon."

"Can I hold her too?" Myrvan asked his sister as the pair started on their way out.

Arianne hesitated for a moment and said, "All right. But don't drop her or anything. And you have to be careful not to hold her too tight."

"It wouldn't be such a big deal if father had made her like us," Myrvan said as he gently took the baby.

"I suppose," said Arianne.

"At least she won't be stupid like the grown-ups," the boy remarked.

"Hey! You shouldn't say stuff like that," she chided him.

"Sorry," he apologized.

"It's not their fault," Arianne added. And as they approached Professor Fournier who was still standing by the door, she stopped and gazed up at him, looking a little embarrassed. "Of course, he doesn't mean you, Professor," she said. "I actually think that both you and Professor Karpov are quite clever … considering."

Fournier raised his eyebrows. *Considering? Considering what?* he wondered. "Uh, thank you … I think," he replied.

Arianne turned to her brother and asked, "Did you say hello to the professor?"

Myrvan looked up. "Hello, Professor."

"Hello, my boy."

The children then continued on their way out.

"Hey, you didn't say hello," Myrvan said to his sister.

"I already saw him earlier," Arianne replied as they left the lab.

Once the children had gone, Fournier proceeded further inside the room. "She takes her role of older sister very seriously," he said.

"Yes, she does," Adam agreed. "It's because of her heightened empathy. She senses how much the others miss having a mother. She's trying to fill that role. At least for her younger brothers and sisters. But she's still too young, herself. She hasn't figured out the best way to do it, yet. Hopefully she will, in time." Adam continued to stare at the closed door a while longer, and then finally turned to Fournier. "Did you want to see me about something, Professor?"

"Yes," said Fournier. "I came to talk to you about Myrvan. I wanted to let you know that he's been hiding his true potential. But it would appear I don't need to, do I?"

Adam's gaze sharpened.

"How long have you known?" The professor asked.

"From the beginning," said Adam. "I'm the one who told him to hold back."

"Why would you do that?" Fournier said, looking perplexed. He pointed at the equations on the whiteboard and added, "I don't think even Damien would have been able to grasp this level of complexity when he was that age."

Adam sighed. "You're right, he wouldn't have … and neither would I."

Fournier's eyes nearly popped out of their sockets. "What are you saying?" he asked, almost whispering.

"To be honest, I'm not sure," Adam replied. "But I'm starting to think that Myrvan might be more gifted than any of us. In more ways than one. If he continues to develop at this rate …"

Professor Fournier was trembling with excitement. "This is incredible."

"Yes, it is," said Adam. "But you can't tell anyone. I'll talk to Professor Karpov. I assume he knows, too."

"Not tell anyone? Why not? This is a major development in the project. It could change everything."

Adam waited a moment to allow Professor Fournier to regain his composure, but also to emphasize the importance of what he was about to say. "Do you remember how most people reacted to me when I was the same age? What was being whispered behind closed doors?"

"Erm … I know there was some apprehension," said Fournier. "But that's understandable. Frankly speaking, no one knew what to make of you."

"It was more than just apprehension," said Adam. "It was fear. Fortunately for me, there was also a great deal of curiosity."

Fournier gave him a probing look. "What are you trying to say?"

"I'm saying there were those who wanted to see me locked away for good … or worse. I was protected because there was no one else like me, because I was unique. My children cannot benefit from such a protection. If the truth about Myrvan ever came to light, I worry about what they might do to him. But most of all, I worry about what he might become if they push him too far."

Chapter 19 – Escape

The living room had fallen completely silent.

Professor Fournier marked a long pause and glanced over his attentive audience.

"That conversation took place about seven months before Adam escaped from the Arc," the old man declared.

"I still can't believe he bailed on his kids like that," Sonar commented.

"He didn't have a choice," Fournier said, looking at Arianne and Lucielle. "It was the only way to keep them safe."

"We know, professor," Arianne said as she took Lucielle's hand.

"You told us he had found out about some secret organization?" Doc said. "WIAS, was it?"

"Yes," the old man replied. "It goes without saying that Adam was kept under constant surveillance at the Arc facility. His every move inside the compound was closely monitored, his living quarters were bugged, and all contact with the outside world was carefully supervised. The only place he could find any privacy was inside his lab. How could he possibly have hoped to expose WIAS under those circumstances? How could he have safeguarded his children against their looming threat?"

"I guess it makes sense," said Doc.

"I'm sure the decision to leave was a terribly difficult one for him to make," said Fournier. "But not only did it give him the freedom to act, it also prompted an increase in security around his children. Adam knew it would keep them out of WIAS's reach for some time."

"And it worked, right?" Kincade asked.

"Yes, it did," Fournier confirmed. "Unfortunately, not even Adam had predicted what was to happen next. The second week after his father's disappearance, Myrvan escaped from the Arc."

The professor's statement was met with shocked gazes and raised eyebrows.

"And how exactly did he manage that?" Doc asked.

A hint of pride flashed across Fournier's face as he replied. "He built a device capable of opening most electronic locks and used it to pass through the restricted areas."

"It was the first prototype of the device we used to get inside the storage room in Leicester's office," Arianne told Kincade.

"What about the cameras?" Doc inquired.

"The day before," Fournier said. "At around the same time he planned to escape, Myrvan intercepted and recorded the camera feeds along the route he intended to take. The following day, he accessed a control panel, hacked into the surveillance system, and replaced the live feeds with the recordings."

"Hehe, not bad," Rock chuckled.

"And the guards?" Kincade asked.

"He had memorized their positions and patrol patterns," Fournier replied. "It wasn't hard for him to avoid most of them. And the ones he couldn't avoid, he simply knocked out. He made his way to an elevator shaft and climbed up the cables all the way to the third floor."

"Why the third floor?" Sonar asked.

"He knew security inside the lobby would be much tighter," the professor explained. "And a higher floor provided a better view of the surrounding area."

"Wow, he really thought this through, didn't he?" said the redhead.

"He did," said Fournier. "But he couldn't have known that the military had installed motion sensors in the yard following Adam's escape. As soon as the boy landed on the ground, the alarm went off."

"Landed?" Doc noted.

"Yes, he jumped from a window," Fournier replied in a matter-of-fact tone.

"Oh," Doc simply said.

Neither the mercenaries nor the detective had a problem accepting that part of Fournier's account. They had all seen enough not to be bothered by this kind of statement anymore.

The professor carried on. "The cameras captured the boy as he ran across the field, moving at an incredible speed I might add. He had also taken the precaution of wearing high-voltage insulating gloves, which he used to rip open the electric fence before he disappeared inside the forest."

"He actually made it out?" Kincade exclaimed in surprise.

"Oh, yes. But he ran into a military patrol car. They slowed him down long enough for the search party from the Arc to catch up. Myrvan was eventually subdued and brought back to the compound." The old man marked another pause, seeming to hesitate. "I should mention … they died," he finally said.

"Who died?" Sonar asked.

"The patrol team," Fournier replied. "All four of them. It was a regrettable accident."

"Accident?" Rock echoed, with clear skepticism in his voice.

"I don't believe Myrvan meant for it to go that far," Fournier argued. "But between the fear of getting caught, and the desperation to find his father … anyone would have found it difficult to exercise restraint in these conditions, especially a child."

Kincade cocked his head to the side. "A child? Wait, how old was he?"

"It was about a month shy of his twelfth birthday," the professor replied.

A grave silence filled the room once again.

The mercenaries exchanged uneasy glances as they tried to imagine a child, not much older than Lucielle, planning and executing such an escape, and then killing four armed soldiers in the process. If nothing else, it gave them a clear illustration of the kind of threat they had allowed in their midst.

"After that night," Fournier continued, not noticing the shift in his audience's mood. "The children's lives dramatically changed. With his near-escape, Myrvan had shown himself to be far more capable than anyone at the Arc realized. But also, far more dangerous. It was just as Adam had feared. Expectations quickly gave way to suspicions, and curiosity turned into concern. The children were no longer allowed to move freely around the facility's sub-levels, their outside privileges were revoked, and everything they did was even more closely monitored. They truly became prisoners."

The old man paused as he tried to recall the subsequent months in clear detail.

"Two weeks later," he said. "A new team was brought in to perform a different kind of '*study*' on the children. The team's lead scientist, a man named Whitmore, was a particularly objectionable fellow.

Their experiments were designed to measure things like pain tolerance levels, or performance under physical stress and sleep deprivation."

"That sounds a bit extreme," Doc remarked.

"It was barbaric!" Fournier exclaimed, still seething at the mere thought of those sessions. "And Myrvan suffered the worst of it. Now that his secret was out, the primary focus shifted away from Damien and onto him. They decided to isolate him and run a series of special tests in order to determine his true capabilities. But the boy refused to cooperate. Like Mitsuki, he too had always been very unresponsive. His new situation, coupled with the disappearance of Adam, only served to reinforced this behavior. The harder they pressed him, the more he retreated within himself. They weren't getting anywhere. So, Whitmore and a couple of his colleagues advocated for even more drastic measures."

"What measures?" Kincade asked.

Fournier lowered his eyes.

"They tortured him," Arianne suddenly declared.

Everyone turned to her.

"They tortured a kid?" said Kincade.

Professor Fournier bowed his head in shame.

"For nearly two years, my brother was subjected to the unimaginable," said Arianne. The anger and revulsion in her voice could be felt by everyone inside the room. She turned to Fournier and added, "It wasn't your fault, Professor. If it hadn't been for you and Professor Karpov, the rest of us would have received a similar treatment."

The old man forced a smile as he gazed at her with teary eyes.

Arianne smiled back. But as she stared at the professor, she decided it was best to give him a little time to collect himself.

"On the rare occasions I was allowed to visit my brother," she said. "I pleaded with him to put an end to it. What did it matter? We had spent our entire lives undergoing tests and running simulations for those same people. I just didn't want him to suffer anymore."

"Did you know about your brother's secret prior to all of this?" Doc asked.

"Of course I did," Arianne replied. "So did the others."

"I see," Doc said.

"What happened next?" Sonar asked.

"I reminded my brother that people were afraid of the unknown, of what they didn't understand," said Arianne. "And that showing himself to be so determined, so uncompromising, was only making him scarier in their eyes. He chose not to listen. He didn't even try to explain it to me. In fact, Myrvan didn't speak at all during those two years."

Kincade closely observed Arianne as she recounted those harrowing events of her youth. He imagined that at times like these her heightened empathic sense must have felt more like a curse than a gift. "It must have been hard for you, too," he said.

"It was unbearable," she said, holding back her tears. "Many times, I contemplated rescuing my brother. Or at least trying."

"Did you? Try, I mean."

"No. I was too worried about the consequences for the others. Even if I had succeeded, what would have happened to them? I realized if we were to escape, we would have to do it together. All of us. But it wasn't possible, then. Not while Lucielle was still a baby." Arianne exhaled deeply. "I was desperate to find a way to help my brother. We all were. But, in the end, we didn't need to."

She glanced at the professor, signaling that he should take over from there.

"One day," said Fournier. "During a routine check-up, I asked Myrvan how he felt. I had gotten into the habit of asking him that question, even though I had long stopped expecting a reply. But that time, he did reply. Not only that, he replied with a sarcastic comment. I was flabbergasted."

"I don't see why that's a big deal," said Rock.

"I understand it may seem trivial to you," the professor said. "But that's because you don't know what Myrvan was like. He was very quiet, and mostly kept to himself. But most of all, he was always dreadfully serious. He almost never smiled. And not once had I seen him even try to be funny. Sarcasm? No, that wasn't at all like him. But at the time, I was so relieved to hear him speak again that I didn't pay enough attention to this change in behavior. And I was even more relieved when he said he'd agree to cooperate. I remember Whitmore and his acolytes being quite pleased with themselves. The project would finally benefit from the participation of its most promising subject."

The old man paused briefly.

"In retrospect," he said. "I should have known right away that there was more to it. But it was only when Arianne was allowed to visit her brother again that it all became clear." Professor Fournier turned to the young woman. "It was an odd scene. She walked into the room and stopped immediately. Neither of them had said a word, yet. She scrutinized her brother for … five to ten seconds, and then asked, *What's your name?'* to which he replied, *'Soran'*."

The old man broke out in laughter.

"Can you imagine the looks on our faces?" he said. "Alek and I immediately understood what had happened. But believe me, the same could not be said of our colleagues. I don't think I've ever seen anyone look so baffled."

He laughed again with renewed exuberance.

"If he didn't speak, how could you tell he was different?" Doc asked Arianne.

"I don't know," she said. "He just … he didn't feel like the person I knew."

"And that's exactly what she told us," the old man continued. "Of course, the other scientists refused to believe it. Especially Whitmore. He dismissed the idea offhand. He was convinced it was a ploy. He even accused Arianne of being the instigator. Bloody fool," Fournier concluded, demonstrating it was possible to sum up one's opinion of another person in no more than two words.

"What happened after that?" Kincade asked.

"The boy cooperated," said Fournier. "The only problem was that all his test results remained more or less within their previous range."

"I'm guessing they accused him of faking it?" said Kincade.

"You guessed correctly," the old man replied. "And to prove it, they ran every test imaginable. But the results were irrefutable. He wasn't 'faking it', as you put it. And the biggest surprise was, by far, his brain scan."

Sonar gave a strange look and said, "You scanned his brain?"

"Of course!" Fournier exclaimed. "Among the litany of tests the children had undergone since birth, brain scans were of paramount importance. We were looking for any clues to help us understand the reason for their superior intelligence. Anyway, the point is, Soran's brain scan was nothing like the ones taken from Myrvan. This was a truly shocking observation. They even brought back the psychiatrists who had examined him when he was younger. Their findings were conclusive, and unanimous: He was not the same person. In the face of this mounting evidence, even Whitmore was forced to accept the facts. And since his team's *services* were no longer required. Alek and I recommended they be expelled from the facility."

"And your recommendation was followed?" Doc asked, surprised.

"Without hesitation," said Fournier. "Whitmore wasn't well-liked by the other Arc scientists, either. And the higher-ups blamed him and his colleagues for the boy's DID—Dissociative Identity Disorder—resulting in the loss of potentially their most valuable asset."

"Were they right?" Doc asked. "Was Soran's condition the result of everything he had endured during those two years?"

The old man gave a coy smile. "That's what Arianne, Alek, and I let them think, because it ensured Whitmore's dismissal. But no, that wasn't the real cause. As I mentioned earlier, each child suffered from some type of psychological disorder. Myrvan was no exception. No doubt his ordeal served as a catalyst which precipitated his personality split. But it would have happened regardless. I think that's what Adam was trying to tell me, that day … inside his lab."

As he recalled the rest of his conversation with Adam, Professor Fournier began to slowly drift away, absorbed in his memories.

"Professor?" Doc said.

"Hmm? Oh, sorry. Where was I? Erm … Yes. The children were never psychologically stable to begin with. Though, some of them did improve considerably with age. But in Myrvan's case … his disdain for people, his rejection of them, was so pronounced that we always feared it would ultimately lead to a radical change. The emergence of a new personality was actually a best-case scenario."

Sonar squinted at the professor and said, "I think you and I have very different ideas about what a best-case scenario is supposed to look like."

"Oh, it could have been much worse," said Fournier. "You see, despite Myrvan's calm exterior, from a very young age, he had been struggling to contain what Adam described as *surges of violent impulses*. It was his relationship with Adam, and also Arianne, that enabled the boy to maintain control, and to keep those urges in check. Both of them acted as tethers, that prevented him from getting swept away by this torrent of violence."

"I guess I can understand about his dad," said Kincade. "But why you?" he asked, turning to Arianne. "Why not his other brothers and sisters?"

"I don't know," she replied.

"I'm not sure, either," said Fournier. "But aside from his father, Arianne's the only person who ever had any sway over Myrvan. But, with Adam gone, and with the boy isolated from his sister, he had effectively lost both of his anchors. That's what caused him to gradually turn into the person you saw. But, of course, the two years of mistreatment exacerbated his condition, and made those violent impulses even stronger. When Myrvan realized what was happening to him, I believe the lingering influence of his father and his sister prompted him to find a way to protect those close to him. Since he couldn't get rid of those urges, he buried them deep inside his own psyche, along with himself. He never really wanted anything to do with other people, anyway. That's when the Soran persona first appeared. And in all the years since, Myrvan hasn't emerged more than a dozen times. It takes a lot to force him out. Like an extremely perilous situation, or a highly traumatic event. You see, it's not a case of two personalities vying to rise to the surface. On the contrary, one of them wants to come out, but the other one does not."

That was it. The professor had reached the end of his tale. But his audience remained focused on him, immobile, and silent.

It was a lot to absorb at once, a lot to process.

Coincidentally, that was when Soran returned to the living room, accompanied by Ashrem, who was visibly still in pain.

"You need to rest," Arianne told the injured man.

"I'll be fine," Ashrem replied.

Kincade could hear a deep concern in the young woman's voice. He thought about the special bond the professor had mentioned, between her and Ashrem. And about the fact that they shared a lot of the same DNA. *Yeah, that's not weird at all,* he said to himself.

Meanwhile, the others were more focused on Soran.

Learning about the young man's past had caused them to see him through different eyes. They weren't naïve enough to fool themselves into thinking it somehow made him less of a threat. If anything, it was the opposite. The professor's account had given them an even greater understanding of the danger he posed. But, it had also given them an added perspective. It was as Arianne had said: people tend to fear what they don't understand. And they understood him a little better, now. They were also reasonably convinced it would take a unique set of circumstances for his other personality to surface again. After all, despite getting shot at, on two separate occasions—at the hotel and at the professor's home—Soran had remained himself.

As the young man walked into the room, Kincade glanced over the faces of his comrades. He was relieved to see that their hard expressions had softened, and that their cold stares had grown warmer.

But curiously, it was actually Soran and his siblings whose eyes glistened with a fierce intensity. They all turned to Fournier.

"You know what we want to ask you, Professor," Ashrem said.

Marie felt the mood inside the room turn heavy once again. The mercenaries didn't say a word, but they too were now eyeing the old man with avid interest. The detective realized she was the only one who had no idea what Ashrem meant. But she didn't dare break this grave silence.

Arianne locked eyes with the professor and said, "Jenkins. Who is he?"

After a long and deliberate pause, Fournier replied, "His real name is Jack."

Chapter 20 – Jack Griffin

Patrick Jenkins stood in front of a hangar at an airfield near Paris, surveying the quiet night sky.

He checked the time on his cell phone.

Seven more minutes had passed.

As he put the phone back inside his jacket's pocket, he heard a sound in the distance. He gazed up and probed the horizon.

A small airplane—a twin-engine private jet—appeared from behind the clouds.

"Finally," Jenkins muttered to himself.

Moments later, the pilot touched down on the deserted runway and then taxied the plane into the hangar bay, under Jenkins' watchful eye.

After the aircraft had come to a complete stop, a man in a black suit exited the cabin and jogged towards to Jenkins.

"Any incidents during the flight?" Jenkins asked as he walked into the hangar.

"None of note, sir," the man replied. "But *our guest* complained the entire time."

"Where is he?"

The man seemed uneasy. "He's still in his seat. He refuses to come out."

Jenkins frowned. "Why not?"

"He said he won't move until he speaks to whoever's in charge," the man in the suit replied. But sensing Jenkins' growing impatience, he quickly added, "You told us to avoid getting rough with him."

"Bring him out," Jenkins growled. "Now."

"Right away, sir. Erm … and if he continues to be difficult?"

Jenkins glared at his subordinate. "Insist."

"Yes, sir," the man said. Eager to put some distance between himself and Jenkins, he hurried back towards the plane as he pressed on his earpiece. "Escort him out.

…

I don't care. Drag him if you have to," the man ordered as he shot a worried glance behind him.

Within seconds, an older man wearing a mahogany sweater and khaki trousers was forced out of the plane. He had a big scar on the right side of his face—starting on his forehead and running half-way down his cheek.

Another man in black emerged from the cabin and shoved the old man down the ramp, all the while ignoring his shouts of protest.

The old man eventually spotted three dark SUVs, parked at the end of the hangar. "What is this?" he bellowed. "Where are you taking me now?"

"Calm down, Whitmore," said Jenkins as he approached from the hangar entrance. "You've caused enough trouble as it is. Your tantrums are making me fall behind schedule."

Whitmore was gobsmacked. "Jenkins ..." he muttered. He stared wide-eyed at Leicester's associate for a long time, and then suddenly became indignant. "*I* caused trouble? Your men abducted me from my home, and flew me across the Atlantic. What's the meaning of this?"

"Come with me," Jenkins simply replied as he headed towards the SUVs.

Whitmore glanced around, and then reluctantly followed him.

When they reached the first vehicle, Jenkins nodded to the driver, who had been waiting outside, and the man promptly opened the back passenger-side door.

"Where are you planning to take me?" Whitmore asked.

"Have a look inside," Jenkins told him.

The old man eyed him suspiciously before he moved closer to the vehicle and peered inside.

He froze instantly.

A flurry of emotions erupted inside Whitmore. How he had longed for this day to come. How many times had he lain awake at night, fantasizing about this very moment? And now, just like that, there she was, tied up and unconscious, in the back seat of a car.

Mitsuki.

"Ooh, Mr. Jenkins," Whitmore purred, unable to pull his gaze away from the young woman. "Please tell me this means what I think it means."

"It does," said Jenkins. "I'm offering you the opportunity to study her once again. And this time, you'll have free rein to run all your twisted experiments."

Whitmore's entire body was shaking with excitement. He took out a prescription vial from his trousers' pocket, opened it, and swallowed two pills. "Nobody looking over my shoulders?" he asked as he ran his fingers up and down his scar.

"That's right. But there's one question in particular to which we'll need the answer."

"Who's '*we*'?"

"Are you in, or not?" Jenkins asked.

Whitmore made a clicking sound with his tongue and cracked a disturbing smile. "Mr. Jenkins, I'll agree to anything you want. Anything at all."

"Good," said Jenkins. "You leave immediately. My men will fill you in on the way. I have to get going."

"Yes, yes, of course," said Whitmore, who was barely listening. But as he leaned closer to the prisoner, his expression changed. "What's this?" he asked, noticing a bruise on Mitsuki's face. He hadn't seen it before because it was mostly covered by her long black hair. He began to inspect her further. There were scrapes on her hands, a cut on her lip, and she probably had other injuries underneath her skin-tight black outfit. "Did you do this?" he asked, glaring at Jenkins.

Jenkins said nothing.

"Was it really necessary?" Whitmore asked. "How badly is she hurt?"

Jenkins was amazed to see that Whitmore seemed genuinely upset. "Why do you care?" he said. "You, of all people. From what I've heard, you did far worse to them during your time at the Arc. And they were only children, then."

"Mr. Jenkins," Whitmore said in an aggrieved tone. "I would thank you not to compare my research to your gratuitous violence. Everything I did, I did in the name of science."

"I doubt that was of any consolation to them," Jenkins scoffed. He then checked the time on his phone again and said, "I'll be in touch."

With that, Jenkins climbed into one of the other SUVs and drove off, leaving Whitmore with his men. And with Mitsuki.

"He's one of the four, isn't he?" said Arianne. "He's the right age. And it's the only explanation I can come up with that makes sense."

"He is," Professor Fournier replied.

Rock gave them a confused look. "One of the four what?"

"Professor Engel's original experiment," said Fournier. "If you recall, I told you that four subjects survived. Adam and three others. Jack Griffin is one of them."

"Wait a minute, he's like them?" Rock asked, pointing at the siblings.

Lucielle frowned at the giant. "That's not what he said."

Fournier shook his head. "No, he's not a clone. But like them, he too was genetically enhanced."

"Why didn't you tell us about him sooner?" Arianne asked the professor.

"I'm sorry," said the old man. "I only realized it after what happened with Ashrem."

"About that," said Rock. "How come Jenkins wiped the floor with him like that? I mean, if they're both *enhanced*, and all."

Sonar raised an eyebrow at his comrade and said, "Weren't you there, too?"

"That's not the point," the giant fired back.

"It's really not that surprising," said Fournier. "Jack's a soldier. His training, his instincts, everything about him has been honed for that purpose. Not only that, but as one of the original four, he would be noticeably stronger than Ashrem. It would take the likes of Darius or Damien to compete with him physically." Fournier turned to the injured young man with an affectionate smile. "There's also the fact that Ashrem abhors violence in all its forms. Even as a child, he could never bring himself to really hurt other people. Not even to defend himself. The only time he ever reacted in anger was to help his younger sister."

Rock gave Ashrem a disapproving frown. "Now that's just plain stupid, dude. That guy could have killed you."

"He's right, you know," Soran agreed. "Those injuries were pretty serious, Ash. You had us all worried, for a minute there."

The giant turned to Soran with an expression of disbelief. "Are you kidding me?" he said. "No, really. Are you kidding me, right now?"

"What?" Soran asked.

"Part of the reason he's in such a bad shape … is *you*," Rock said, pointing a finger at the young man.

Soran lowered his eyes. "You're right. I'm sorry, Ash."

Ashrem smiled at his younger brother. "It's all right. It wasn't your fault." He then turned to the professor and said, "There was something else I wanted to ask you about Jenkins."

"What's that?" said Fournier.

"When we fought," Ashrem said. "He had this look in his eyes. It wasn't just about his mission. I felt a deep anger. A hatred, even. Why would he harbor such strong feelings towards me?"

Fournier ran his hand over his head. "Hmm … I think his grievance is not so much with you, but rather with your father."

"Our father?" Arianne echoed. "Why? What did he do?"

"Nothing," said the old man. "Well, not directly, anyway. You see, Jack was always very … antagonistic towards Adam. He had a profound distrust and dislike for him."

"Did something happen between them?" Ashrem asked.

"No, it's more complicated than that," Fournier replied. "It started when they were very young. I think Jack could always sense that Adam was hiding something. Even back when the rest of us thought the only difference between him and the other three children was his strange hair color. So when Adam's secret came to light, Jack felt vindicated. In his eyes, it validated all his mistrust and hostility. And to make matters worse, Jack's status had changed, along with that of the other two subjects. It must have felt like everyone had stopped focusing on all the gifts they possessed, and instead, judged them based on the one they lacked: Adam's vastly superior intelligence. In the end, the three of them were treated as bargaining chips in the negotiations over who would get custody of Adam. And as a result of those negotiations, Jack was handed over to the US military. That was the last time I saw him." Fournier marked a pause as he searched his memory. "Later on, I got wind of an incident involving Jack. But I was never able to find out any of the details. The truth is, I have no idea what happened to him after he was taken away. To think that after all these years, he would return to the Arc as Patrick Jenkins, head of security ..."

"That still doesn't explain why he went all psycho on Ashrem," Rock pointed out.

"In the time preceding his departure for the US, Jack's resentment towards Adam had grown even more intense," said Fournier. "It's possible something fuelled this sentiment over the years. And now that Adam's gone, Jack's hatred for him may have shifted to his children. Not just Ashrem, but all of them," the professor emphasized as he cast an eye over the four siblings.

"I always felt uncomfortable around Jenkins," Arianne remarked. "Now I know why."

"Hehe! Tough luck," said Rock. "I guess you guys aren't going to make it on his Christmas list."

"Everything OK, Doc?" Kincade asked, noticing his comrade had been staring into space for the past few seconds.

"Huh? What?" Doc said, a little startled.

"You seem to be somewhere else," said Kincade.

"Oh, it's just that … all this talk about Jenkins reminded me of something," Doc said. He paused and glanced around the room. "I guess now is as good a time as any to mention it."

Everyone turned to him, intrigued.

"I didn't stop to think about it at the time because of all the bullets flying around," said Doc. "But something curious happened while Da Costa and I were trapped in that hotel kitchen. When Carson barged in, he was genuinely surprised to find us there. Quite frankly, I'm kind of impressed at the way he managed to fight us off, afterwards. But the look on his face when he first showed up was unmistakable. It was shock."

"What's your point?" Rock asked.

"Don't you get it?" Soran said. "That *is* the point. The fact that Carson didn't know they were pinned down in the kitchen, leaves us with only one possible conclusion: he wasn't in contact with the snipers on the outside."

"Exactly," said Doc.

Rock suddenly looked even more confused. "But Ashrem and I had a run-in with those guys, after

Jenkins blew up our tire and crashed our van. They were definitely following his orders."

"Isn't Carson supposed to be teaming up with Jenkins?" Sonar asked.

"He is," Arianne said, wearing a pensive frown. "It's quite strange."

"An oversight, maybe?" the redhead suggested.

"I guess it's possible that, in all the commotion, there was a mix-up in communications," Soran said. "But that doesn't seem very likely."

"Indeed," Ashrem concurred. "It sounds more like Jenkins is keeping secrets from Carson. But why?"

The living room fell silent once again as everyone stopped to ponder this strange new development.

"Well," Kincade eventually said. "Clearly, this Jenkins character is more complicated than we realized. But we'll worry about him when the time comes." He cast an eye over the entire group and added, "I think we've all had enough excitement for one day. We can pick this up tomorrow."

"Good idea," Fournier agreed. "It *has* been an eventful day. I'm sure everyone's tired. Please, make yourselves at home. There should be enough space. Though, someone will probably have to take the sleeping couch," he said, nodding to the large sofa.

"I'll crash on the couch," said Kincade. He then turned to his comrade. "Sonar, you take first watch. I'll relieve you in a bit."

"Understood," said the redhead.

The professor gave a surprised look. "First watch? That won't be necessary. I assure you, no one knows about this place. You don't have to worry about Leicester's men showing up in the middle of the night."

"That's not what we're worried about," Rock said, eyeing Soran.

"Oh, come on," the young man complained. "I'm really sorry, OK? Can we get past this, already?"

"Ask me again in a year or two," said the giant.

Soran muttered something unintelligible as he and Ashrem headed back to their rooms.

Fournier watched them walk away, and then approached the detective. "Please, come with me," he said. "I'll show you to your room."

"Thank you," Marie said.

She followed the professor deeper into the apartment, accompanied by Arianne and Lucielle.

With his team getting ready to turn in as well, Kincade pulled Doc Chen aside and said in a low voice, "About that talk you wanted to have ..."

"It's fine," said Doc. "It'll wait until tomorrow. The professor's right. We're all exhausted."

"All right," said Kincade. "Tomorrow, then."

www.ingramcontent.com/pod-product-compliance
Lightning Source LLC
Chambersburg PA
CBHW052042240626
47153CB00006B/2192